RELENTLESS
TEARS

RELENTLESS
TEARS

KAHINI H. TRIFFO

ISBN: 978-1-4269-6288-2 (sc)
ISBN: 978-1-4269-6289-9 (e)

Trafford rev. 04/19/2011

 www.trafford.com

North America & International
toll-free: 1 888 232 4444 (USA & Canada)
phone: 250 383 6864 ♦ fax: 812 355 4082

Life is like a drama-filled novel you don't know what's going to happen the next day or the next second. You meet people; they become friends. You meet more people; they become enemies. You meet the one best friend in your life that helps you with the pain that your mom puts on you almost every night, and you lose him or her in a second and wish you could go back in the past and change whatever you did for you guys not to be friends anymore. Then, you meet that person that knows everything about you and understands how you feel. Then, you make mistakes and say the wrong things, and you lose him or her, just like that! In one heartbeat. You try to get him or her back, but you can't; he or she doesn't care. He or she just wants to be done with you.

The worst of all: you lose your brother, your best friend, and he's never coming back because he's gone ... forever; you cry and plead, but it doesn't change anything. Your life is ruined, your brother will never be by your side again, and the two people you loved don't want anything to do with you. You feel as if chunks of your heart have been ripped out, and you can't make it feel better ever. It feels as though it's going to hurt forever. You miss them, want them back, but they don't feel the same for you; you wish you could go back and change everything ... Can you?

TABLE OF CONTENTS

Chapter 1: **A Girl Named Marina**

Hi, my name is Jenny Fortella, and my life is gone. There's nothing to look forward to anymore; there's nothing to enjoy; there's just me. How did this all start?

"Hey, Jenny."
"Hey, Rebecca, how are you?"
"I'm fine," she said to me as she walked away to her emo friends.

Today was actually starting to be a good day, but I couldn't say for sure yet; it was only first period. It was the beginning of the school year, and everybody was trying to figure out what cliques they were in, and there were so many including the Goth, the Preps, the unknown and many of the so called ghetto at Brownsville Middle School.

"This is your last year of middle school; you better make the best of it," my mom would tell me every day before I left for the bus stop. I didn't pay much attention, though. School was okay, I guess; I had friends, but not that kind of best friend in the whole world who I could tell everything to. I wish I did, though. I was a part of the normal group, not the most popular kids in school, but not the nerdish kids that picked their noses at lunch and discussed the different colors. My classes were all advanced because of my mom's choice to put me in them because I'm so smart; I think it's because she wants to torture me. The guys there were average looking, I guess, and I had no enemies or bullies so far. I met a girl named Marina; she sat behind me in gym (the only class I had that wasn't advanced, but if there were such a thing as advanced gym, I bet my mom would put me in that, too).

"I like your hair," Marina said to me.

"Why?" I asked, shocked.

"Ummm, because it's curly and long; you should straighten it."

"Tried that before, and it didn't work out so well."

"Oh, what happened?"

"Let's just say I looked like a poodle," I said to her.

"It couldn't have been that bad," she said to me with a smile, trying to make me feel better.

Marina was a very pretty person who all the guys liked. She had long, dark brown almost black hair with side bangs, and it was always straight and shiny. She was, biracial so when her hair got wet, she would freak. She was also going out with a guy named Drake. He was tall, muscular (but not too muscular), with dark blond curly hair and hazel eyes. He's one of the okay-looking guys on my list ... Well, actually, he's very good looking. Marina was very nice, unlike those other preppy girls who think they know everything and think they can boss everyone around. She was different, but a good different. I liked it. Marina and I talked the whole forty-five minutes of gym. We talked about our families, boys, and school. I liked talking to her. It's as if she understood me, and I understood her, too! It was great. Who knew that this girl Marina Michelle Santio would become my best friend, for a while?

"Binnnnnnnnnnnnnggg."

2

"There's the bell," Marina said.

"Yeah, I know. Ughh, it's so hot outside; why do we have to have gym second period?"

"I know, right? I'd rather have this class last," she said.

"Ha ha, me, too," I laughed.

"Hey, what class do you have next?" she asked me as we were walking up the stairs.

"Advanced Science," I said back, trying to catch my breath.

"Really? Me too!"

"That's really cool."

"Yeah, I know … hey, walk with me to my locker, and we'll go together, okay?"

"Yeah, sure," I answered.

As we walked to class, people looked at me and smiled. I knew it was only because I was with Marina, but I didn't really care; I kind of liked the attention. As we walked hall by hall, we finally came to our class. "Mrs. Switsull" was the name on the door.

"What kind of name is 'Switsull'?" Marina chuckled.

"I don't know, but I guess we're about to find out." I laughed as I opened the door to science.

We walked in and found two empty seats and sat down. Science was my favorite subject; it was so easy for me, and it looked as if it was for Marina, too. She passed me a note that said, "Hey, call me: 727-867-9045." I smiled and nodded. After the bell rang, it was time for lunch. I usually sat with a girl named Julie who never talks, but today, I wanted to sit with Marina. I didn't ask, though; I didn't want to seem as if I was pushing myself on her, so I just walked away and went to my locker. She ran behind me and said, "You're sitting with us at lunch, right?"

"Umm, if you want," I answered.

"No, duh, I want you to sit with me, or I wouldn't be asking." She laughed.

"Ha ha, okay," I replied as I shut my locker.

The table she sat at was filled with preppy blondes or brunettes and tall cute guys; one of them specifically stood out to me. His name was Jeremiah. He was tall, thin, and his skin was so smooth it glistened; he was light brown but more of a mocha color, with dark brown hair and hazel eyes. I thought to myself, *How can I feel so safe by looking at a guy for about four to five seconds; how could I feel as if I wanted to smile and jump up and down for a long time; how could this one guy make me feel as if everything in the world was okay, right when I looked at him?*

"Come on, Jenny!" Marina yelled as she walked into the line.

"Oh ... I'm coming."

I snapped out of my daydream and quickly realized I was in the real world. I walked slowly in the line, thinking about him with a smile on my face. Marina looked at me, and all I could think was *This is a start of a new beginning.*

Chapter 2: **"I'm sorry; I'm sorry; I'm sorry"**

"What are you going to get?" she asked as she put a salad on her tray.

See, Marina was the type of person that watched her weight a lot. And I wasn't, so I said, "A cheeseburger."

She looked at me, disgusted, and said, "Okay." I smiled and looked away.

"So, I saw you looking at J; what was that about?" she asked. *J? Who's J?* I asked myself ... I thought for a second, and when I finally came to my senses and figured out she was talking about Jeremiah, I started to blush so hard that you would think that I was getting ready to throw up.

"Do you like him?" she finally came out and asked.

"Umm, no?" I answered. "I mean, I think he's cute and everything, but I don't like him," I added.

"Oh, okay ... I just wanted to ask," she said.

"Well, why did you want to ask; does it look like I do?"

"No, I just thought you did because you were, like, staring at him," she said, laughing.

"Oh ..."

As we walked to the table, Jeremiah started looking at me. I put my head down quickly, before he saw me looking at him.

When we got to the table, Marina sat right next to Drake, of course.

I had a couple of classes left until the day was over, and of course, none of those classes were with Marina. As soon as I knew it, though, it was time to leave and go home. Sometimes, I wish school could be all day so I wouldn't have to go home. I don't like being home; my parents are always fighting, and my mom is horrible. She treats my siblings better than she does me. She always yells at me, curses me out, and makes me feel like crap. She calls me ugly, stupid, dumpy, and a lot more (but I'd rather not say). Sometimes, I just cry and cry the whole night, looking up into the sky asking God what I did to her for her to hate me so much. Sometimes I just wish I was dead, that I had no feelings in my heart and soul, because I can't take the hurt and pain. I just couldn't take feeling the way I did every second of the day. I wanted her to love me, to care for me, and most of all, not to beat me, but I knew that that wish would absolutely never come true. I walked home in the heat, opening the door of my two-story house with balconies and pools in Miami, Florida. My dad was a lawyer, and my mom was a nurse. The first thing that ran up to me when I walked through the door was Scrappy, my caring dog. I bent over as he licked my face. My two brothers and sister—Henry, Johnny, and Katelyn—came up to me to say hi (Johnny was the only one who gave me a hug). I said hi back like a hurt puppy. My older brother, Henry, who was in the eleventh grade, asked me what was wrong.

"Is Mom home?" I asked.

"No, she went to the store," Katelyn answered.

"Oh," I said and walked away.

"Why does it matter if she is home or not?" she asked.

"Nothing, I just wanted to make sure she wasn't home."

"*Why!* What is your problem with Mom, Jenny? Why do you hate her so much?" she yelled.

Ugh, she doesn't understand; none of them do! So why can't she just stay out of my life, I thought to myself. I walked to the kitchen to get something to eat, still not answering my sister's questions. She followed me around and kept saying the same thing over and over and over.

"Why do you hate Mom ... why do you hate Mom ... why do you hate Mom!"

I rolled my eyes and ignored her for as long as I could. I walked up the stairs with a Pop-Tart in my hand and a Sprite in the other. She kept babbling on and on and on about how I shouldn't hate my mother because she gave birth to me and blah, blah, blah. I finally couldn't take it anymore, so I turned around and screamed, "Shut up! You don't know what you're talking about! If you would be home when just your mother and I are home, maybe you would understand why I hate her! So for now, get out of my face and leave me alone!"

I slammed the door in her face and quickly locked it before she could come in and yell at me some more. I sat there on my bed, watching TV, eating my Pop-Tart and thinking of the only good things in my life right now:

1. Jeremiah
2. Marina
3. Johnny

I heard the front door open and the crashing of food in grocery bags. My heart dropped. My mom was home!

"Come put the groceries away!" she screamed up the stairs.

"Coming", I responded, terrified.

I ran down the stairs as fast as possible, trying not to trip and fall on my face. As I saw my mom, I quickly said, "Hi, Mom."

"Hi, Jenny, how was school?"

"F... in ... e," I stuttered.

"Where are your sister and brothers?" she asked.

"Umm, I don't know," I said shyly.

"Since you don't, you can wash your damn hands and bring your butt in this kitchen and cook dinner ... now!" she demanded.

"But what about Katelyn and Henry? Can't they help?" I asked.

"Don't give me your attitude, Jenny!"

"I'm not, Mom; I'm just wondering," I answered.

"Well, you can wonder all you want while you're cooking us dinner."

"Ugh, okay," I whispered.

But somehow she heard, because *bam*! Right across my face, a slap so hard I couldn't feel that side of my face for a second. Tears streamed down my cheeks because of the tingling in my eyes; I couldn't help myself. I wept and started the dinner as she walked away. My little brother walked in and tugged my shirt. He saw my tears and felt my pain. He gave me a hug as I could feel a tear run down his face. I wiped his eyes and kissed his cheek. He smiled, but he still knew what was happening. I was getting abused, and he didn't like it. But this was just the beginning. I turned on the oven as I sprinkled a little more cheese on the top of the pasta and shoved it in the oven at 350 degrees. It would be done in about twenty to thirty minutes. Henry and Katelyn came inside from wherever they were. "Where were you guys!"

I yelled softly so my mom wouldn't hear.

"We were outside playing ball; calm down," Henry said.

"How dare you leave me alone with her in the house!" I screamed.

"Who?" Katelyn yelled.

"Mom," I said.

"Why can't you be home with Mom?" Katelyn asked, frustrated.

"Never mind," I said quickly and ran up the stairs to cry in my room.

I opened the door and closed it and slid down with tears streaming down my face. Today was a better day than usual. I usually cry ten times a day when I come home from school, just because when I'm in this house, I feel trapped in a gas chamber, never able to get out. I feel as if I'm dying. As if every second that I breathe, I'm getting weaker and weaker every minute that I'm alive.

I heard Scrappy screech as the front door flew open. *Crap, I thought to myself. I forgot to put him back in his cage.* My dad hates Scrappy; if he see's him around or inside, he will do anything to hurt him. Kick, shove, step on, and—one time—try to stab him. I ran downstairs and saw him on the floor, not able to move. My dad had shoved scrappy into the wall fiercely. I wept and picked him up, carried him up the stairs, and laid him down on my bed, whispering "I'm so sorry" in his ear.

He whined and tried to lick my face in any possible way that he could. I closed my door and ran downstairs to check on the pasta. It was ready; I cut it into small pieces and set it on the stove. I brought out five dishes and set them around the table; it would have been six, but I decided not to eat tonight. I do that a lot; one time, I didn't eat for three days, but I survived. And it's not as though anyone would miss me at the dinner table (except Johnny), so it didn't matter. When I was done, I rushed up the stairs to take care of Scrappy. I could see him looking up at me while whining. I knelt down beside my bed to see what his injuries were. One of his legs had been sprained, and the other leg had a deep cut. I went to the bathroom and grabbed the doggy first aid kit that I made my uncle buy for me for Christmas in case something like this ever did happen. I grabbed the wet towel to clean the scrape; he screeched louder than ever.

"Shhhhhh," I whispered softly.

He quieted down. I took out the bandage and wrapped it around his leg tightly, but not too tightly, so it could straighten out his bone. I added a different bandage to the other leg.

When I was done, I got one of his doggy bones that I had been saving up for and gave him one. He started to chew; I laid him down in his bed as I started to sing. Singing always calmed him down. I sang to also calm myself down from my misery. He loved it, and so did I. Singing made me feel amazing. It refreshed my soul and heart from all the bad things. It healed my pain. But when I stopped, the pain rushed back in like a river; at some point, it's calm, and then, the big waves and heavy water rush back in.

I heard a knock on my door. I opened it quietly.

"Sissy, come eat." It was Johnny.

"I'm not eating tonight," I said.

"Why?" he said as if he was about to cry.

"Because I can't be with them right now." ("Them" meant my aggressive father and my abusive mother.)

"Why?" he asked again.

"Because it hurts," I said with a tear in my eye. "Do you want Sissy to be hurting?" I added.

"No," he said.

"Okay, then just go back downstairs and eat your food. Just tell them I'm not hungry tonight," I answered.

He turned and walked away as a tear fell from his eye.

"Hey, Johnny," I said quietly. He turned around. I knelt down with my arms open. "I love you," I said. He ran into my arms, crying, whispering, "I love you, too." I wiped his eyes and told him to hurry downstairs; he left my arms and ran. I closed my door and opened my backpack, searching for Marina's number and called her. It rang.

"Hello," she said.

"Hey, it's Jenny."

"Oh, hey!" she replied, as if she was happy to hear from me.

"What's wrong?" she asked hearing the sadness in my voice.

"Nothing," I replied with a sniffle.

"Are you sure? I can tell something's wrong deep down inside," she said sincerely. I began to cry.

"No," I said.

"Oh my goodness, are you okay? What's going on?" She talked to me as if she was so concerned.

As if I was her child and she was trying to protect me (which my mother never did). I don't know why, but I felt as if I could tell her everything that was going on, as if I could pour my heart out to her and she would understand, so I did. It was an amazing feeling, actually telling someone what was going on instead of keeping it inside my heart where it would keep building up until I could just explode. When I was done, all I heard was the sound of her TV in the background.

"Hello ..." I said. "Hello?" I repeated but this time slower.

"Oh, I'm sorry; I didn't hear you."

Oh my God! Marina was crying. I could tell by her voice and the sniffles in her nose. I felt touched; no one has ever cried for me before (except Johnny, but no one that was outside my family).

"Are you crying?" I asked.

"Of course I am; how can you tell a person something like that and not expect her to cry?" she answered. "I'm sorry; I really am," she added.

"It's okay," I said to her to try to calm her down.

"No, it's not, Jenny! You need to tell someone," she demanded.

"*No, I can't!*" I yelled.

I mean, what was this girl thinking? Now I totally regretted telling her. What if she opened her mouth to an administrator or something, and they took me away from my family? This couldn't happen, and it wouldn't happen.

"Why! Are you just going to stay there and keep getting hurt and abused, which you don't deserve?" she yelled again.

11

"I don't know, but I can't and I won't, Marina; I can't leave."

"Why not, Jenny?" she asked, concerned.

"I can't leave Johnny and Scrappy; even though I'm hurting, I would hurt even more if I left them; they're like two of my best friends." I began to cry with fear that she would tell.

"Jenny, don't cry; I'm not going to tell if you really don't want me to. I'm just worried, but I'll always be here for you, no matter what, okay, whenever you need me," she said.

I cried harder. My heart felt love and a little bit healed, as if a warm blanket had covered it, and I wasn't freezing cold anymore. As I hung up the phone, I truly believed that Marina could be one of my best friends. It was 11:30 p.m.; I was so hungry.

I tiptoed downstairs and found three pieces of lasagna left. I picked up one but decided not to warm it; if my mom heard the microwave, who knew what she would do to me for waking her up. I got a drink and began to walk back upstairs. I heard a door open; I was terrified, wondering if it was my mom or not. The footsteps came closer and closer. I closed my eyes and waited. The footsteps stopped. I felt a sigh of relief. I opened my eyes and saw Henry's face right in front of mine.

"Ahhhh!" I screamed. "What is your problem?" I said, slapping him on the arm.

"Ha ha ha, I wasn't trying to scare you; I was coming downstairs to see who was up at 11:30 when they're supposed to be sleeping." He laughed.

"Oh ... well, it's none of your business if I'm up at 11:30," I said, rushing in before he could speak again.

"God, ha ha, someone's PMS-ing," he tried to tease.

"Whatever, just shut up," I whispered and walked back up to my room. Scrappy was already sleeping; everyone in the house usually was sleeping before me. My door opened quietly. It was Johnny.

"Can I sleep with you, Sissy? Henry snores," he said.

"Sure, Johnny," I answered. He climbed in my bed and relaxed in the blanket, and I did the same.

"Can you tell me a story?" he asked.

"Okay."

As I began to start my story, Johnny dosed off and fell asleep. As soon as I saw his eyes close, I turned off my lamp and did the same.

Chapter 3: **The Mistake**

I woke up with Johnny next to me drooling on my hair. I got out of bed slowly so I wouldn't wake him up. (Johnny wasn't a good morning person.) I quickly got into the shower. As I got out, I looked at myself in the mirror, my dark green eyes glistening and sparkling, and my Puerto Rican skin smooth and soft. And my curly brown thick hair down to my ribs. *Should I straighten my hair today?* I asked myself. I went to my bedroom and decided what I was going to wear. I went to my sister's room to get her smooth and shine conditioner that I was *never* allowed to use, but I was taking the risk for a cute day. As I rubbed it into my hair, Johnny came up to me and said "Sissy" over and over again, each time getting louder and louder until he was screaming.

"Sissy, Sissy!"

"Yes!" I yelled.

"What are you doing?" he asked.

Wow, the little child is screaming my name as if he was having a heart attack just to know what I was doing, I thought to myself. I chuckled and answered, "My hair." until I didn't hear him say another word.

I began to straighten my hair, taking each strand one by one straightening it to perfection. About a hour later, I was done.

I brushed out the tangles until it was as smooth as the fresh white sand that you roll in at the beach. I looked at myself in the mirror. *Wow!* I thought to myself. My hair was beautiful! It was shiny and smooth and extremely long! I played with it at first because it's never been this gorgeous in my life! I was amazed, and for the first time, I could stand in front of the mirror and say I was ... beautiful.

I said good-bye to Johnny and kissed him on the forehead, laying him in my bed. As I left the house for school, I told him not to make too much noise or Mom would wake up and be very cranky and probably take it out on me when I got home. I walked out the door looking up and down at my outfit. I was wearing dark blue jeans with a white polo shirt with a black tank top under it. I headed to the bus with my head up, strong and brave, getting ready for a new day.

"Wow, what happened to you?" this kid, John, said to me as I walked past him.

"Umm?" I said shyly.

"It's not a bad—I mean, you don't look bad; I've just never seen your hair straight," he said quickly because he thought he hurt my feelings.

"I know ... and thank you," I said soflty and then smiled.

As the bus pulled up and I got on, I had a smile on my face. And I liked it a lot. When I began to walk down the aisle, I got so many compliments on my hair that I felt so special, and I was the center of attention, for once. People said, "I love your hair!" and "Aw, it looks really good," and one guy even said, "Dang, she looks fine today!"

All I could do was giggle and go to my seat. I got to school feeling more brave and outspoken. I was really happy that day. I felt all bubbly inside, as if I could just scream or jump up and down and not care what anyone else thought. Like a little girl sitting on Santa's lap for the first time.

I walked down the stairs of the bus when we pulled up to the tall blue building. I spotted Marina right when I got off the bus. She took one quick glance at me and screamed.

"OMG, OMG, OMG," she kept saying over and over and over as she felt my hair.

"Do you like it?" I asked.

"*Duh*, ha ha, I love it!" she said with the biggest smile on her face.

After she was done screaming, she gave me a hug, and I could see a tear run down her face.

"I'm so sorry about your situation with your mom Jenny." she kept repeating in a soft voice so no one else would hear and be nosey. The smile I had on my face turned into a frown. I could feel my heart melt with sadness as she hugged me tightly. I wrapped my arms around her and began to sob on her shirt. People walked by us, looking at us crying to each other. Marina just kept repeating, "I'm sorry." When she let go, I felt bad because there was a huge tear stain on her shirt.

She looked at me and wiped my eyes, as I did with Johnny.

"I'm so sorry about your shirt," I told her.

"Don't be; I like it like this," she said, giggling.

As she walked me to my first period class, I sniffled and fixed my hair, as I walked the darkest place in this school ... the halls. I got pushed by some guy that was running. I spun twice and knocked my head on a locker. "*Ouch!*" I screamed. I could barely move, so I just stood there for a couple of seconds. As I turned my head, I saw Jeremiah standing next to me. I looked at him in amazement, and he continued to stand there, looking at the locker I was at. It took me about five seconds to notice the locker I was on was his.

"Oh, I'm sorry," I said while moving. He laughed.

"It's okay," he said to me, looking right into my eyes. I put my head down and kept it there until he asked me, "Are you okay?"

"Um, yeah," I answered quickly.

"Are you sure?" he asked, convinced that something really was wrong.

"Yeah, I'm fine," I kind of said with an attitude and began to walk away.

Where was Marina when I needed her? He ran behind me and said, "Do you want to tell me what's wrong, or am I going to have to keep guessing?"

"Ha ha, you're going to have to keep guessing," I chuckled.

"Okay, are you sick, mad, sad, hurt?" he rambled on.

"No, yeah, yes, and I don't know," I replied.

"Wait, which ones were those again?" he asked, trying to make me laugh, and I did. As we reached my class, I stopped and looked at the door until he got the hint that it was my class.

"Um, I have to go," I said.

He looked at the door and said, "Oh, okay, see you later." I smiled and nodded. And right when he began to walk away, he turned around and said, "By the way, I really like your hair." I smiled and opened the door.

All during my class, I had a smile on my face. I felt as if nothing could ever make it go away. I sat there in history thinking about him and how he was concerned about me. I wondered if he liked me, or if he was just bored so he decided to talk to me. But I convinced myself that he didn't and doesn't, because I really did not want to get my hopes up, and then get them crushed as I usually do. As the bell rang, I jumped out of my seat and ran to the door. As I opened it, I looked both ways to see if Jeremiah was coming. He didn't show up, so I just walked to gym, disappointed.

Running behind me was Marina.

"Hey, where did you go this morning?" she asked, confused.

"I don't know; the crowd of people was so big I got lost in it, I guess," I said to her.

"Oh, okay, did anything happen that I missed?" she asked.

"Umm, nope," I told her, lying through my teeth.

School went by really fast. And I didn't have that much homework. When the bell rang for us to leave, I almost cried. I had to go home to a world of hate, selfishness, and suffering. As I got on the bus, I could hear my mom calling me ugly and stupid, and punching me in the stomach. I could see my parents getting into another fight and blaming it all on me. As I began to think this, my eyes began to water and tears began to fall down my cheeks. *Why, God, why?* I began to think to myself. *Why are you punishing me?* As I got on the bus, I sat in my seat and wished in my heart that this bus would take me far, far away, where only good things happened and no hurt or pain could ever come in. When the bus stopped, I looked out and watched the other kids get off the bus with smiles on their faces. *Can I come home with you?* I wondered to myself. But I knew that would never happen.

When the bus came to a stop, I got off with a tear running down my face. As I got home, there was a crack in the door. I pushed the door open, and right in my face were my mom and sister looking at me with the scariest looks. I knew something bad was going to happen.

"Why did you use my hair cream? Do you know how much a bottle costs?" my sister yelled.

"I—I wanted my hair to look pretty like yours," I stuttered.

"Stay out of my room and out of my stuff!" she yelled in my face.

"O—okay," I stuttered again.

As I watched Katelyn leave the house, I pleaded, *Please, don't leave me*, in my head. As the door closed, my mom looked at me and the pain began.

"How dare you!" she shouted and slammed me on the ground, as she began to hit and scream, "I hate you; why can't you just die!" I looked up at her as she began the punches and I counted. One ... two ... three ... four ... five ... six ... seven. There was blood on the wood floor from my nose, my ears, and the top of my head. I heard the room door open. It was Johnny; as my mom heard the door, she stopped the pain and ran out of the house, leaving me there in my blood.

"Sissy!" he screamed as he ran down the stairs, crying.

"I'm okay; I'm okay," I lied just to make him stop.

I went to the bathroom to see myself in the mirror. I looked horrible; no wonder Johnny wouldn't stop crying. It looked as if half of my face had been ripped off. As I began to clean myself, it hurt so bad that tears ran down my face more than ever before.

When I was done, I struggled to go clean my blood off the floor. I had purple bruises all over me, and the blood would not stop. I had to keep a towel around my face to catch the blood when it came gushing out. When I went to my room, Scrappy was awake and yawning; he looked at me and screeched. I tried to calm him down because I didn't want my dad hearing him when he got home.

As my sister came running inside with my mom behind her, she saw my face, and she screamed.

"What happened to you!" my mom said, trying to act as if she didn't know.

Johnny looked up at her, disgusted, as if he wanted to kill her.

"Oh my goodness, Jenny, what happened?" my sister asked.

Your mother hit me ... hard! That's what happened, I thought to myself. I wanted to say it out loud. But she would just deny it, and later, when no one was looking, she would hurt me even more, so I didn't bother saying anything. I just stood there, blood streaming down my face through the towel.

"Come on, sweetie, let me clean you up," my mom yelled.

She took me to her room and sat me down. She came up to me with these small alcohol patches. She held one on my face; I screamed and began to cry. She looked at me with care on her face, but I knew deep down in her heart she loved to see me in pain. My sister stood by her and looked at me, concerned.

"How did this happen, Jenny?" she asked with tears running down her face.

My mom looked at me: if I told her the truth, she would hurt me even more. I took a deep breath and began to lie.

"I tripped down the stairs and hit my head on the sharp part of the handle," I said to her.

"Oh my God! Thank God you weren't extremely hurt," my sister replied.

I wish I was extremely hurt and died! I thought to myself. When my mom was done, she made me my favorite food, macaroni and cheese with fries and grape juice. When I was finished eating, I wondered if I should call Marina and tell her what happened. But I convinced myself not to; she would probably call the police and have me removed from my family, which I wanted, but then again, didn't want at all.

I was so confused and frustrated. I didn't know what to do anymore. I was tired of living, wished it was my time to die. As Johnny walked into my room, he put his head on my shoulder and began to cry.

"Don't die, Sissy; don't ever die," he pleaded, as if he could read my mind. I looked shocked.

"What! Who told you I wanted to die?" I asked.

"Nobody, I can just tell that you want to," he said back, as if he understood everything in my life.

"I don't want to die, Johnny; I wouldn't be able to see your face every day." I smiled.

He giggled as I tickled him. I leaned forward and kissed him on the forehead, which hurt because I had to move my face, but I didn't show that it did. As he walked out, I tried to lay down on my bed, but every way I tried hurt intensely. But I laid there, thinking to myself, *What am I going to do tomorrow? What am I going to say when people ask? Am I going to tell Marina? Will she figure it out and call the police? And most of all, will Jeremiah ever talk to me again as soon as he sees how I look tomorrow?* All those thoughts came to my mind as I laid there in pain with my eyes closed, head hurting, and bruises aching.

Chapter 4: **I'm here for you**

I woke up aching from the pain my mom left me all over yesterday. As I struggled out of bed, I walked to the mirror to see if I looked any better. Nope ... "Ugh, how the heck am I supposed to go to school looking like this?" I said to myself quietly. I walked to my room to find what I was going to wear. I figured out that I couldn't wear jeans because it hurt too much. So I decided to wear sweats and a black loose T-shirt. I didn't dare set a foot in my sister's room. The thought of walking in there brought pain and suffering to my soul. As I got dressed, I put my hair up with a black ribbon in it. I looked at myself in the mirror again and cried. I looked like a monster. My head was big and puffy, with big black and blue bruises all over. My legs looked as if I had been beaten with a baseball bat. Every time I would walk, my legs trembled, and when I touched my face, I quivered with pain. "What am I going to do?" I cried to Scrappy as he whined in his bed; he hadn't been moving for a while now. He just sat there looking at me, and when I left, he would eat, sleep, drink, and play with his toys until I got home so I could sing to him. I smiled at myself in the mirror, trying to make myself feel a little better.

"Sissy, are you going to school now?" Johnny asked.

"No, not yet, hun, in a little bit, though," I answered him.

"Why do you look so sad?" he asked.

"Because, Johnny, I got beaten yesterday and it hurts ... a lot." I answered not thinking, because if I was, I wouldn't have said that at all.

"You got beaten!" he yelled.

No, Johnny, I just fell on the floor, bleeding automatically, I thought to myself, agitated.

"Johnny, it's okay; Sissy is going to be fine," I said, trying to change the subject.

"No, you're not!" he yelled back.

I walked him to my room, sat him on my bed, and turned on the TV to his favorite cartoons. "Yes, I am," I said, kissing his forehead. A tear fell down his face. I hugged him and said, "Don't worry about me." I walked out of the room, grabbing my backpack.

I didn't think about saying bye to my dad because he wasn't really a great morning person. So I left starting off my day looking like a hurt, lost dog. As I walked to the bus stop, my head was down so no one would see my scars. When I got there I looked up, and everyone looked at me. Their eyes got extremely big, as if they were watching someone die. I put my head down and walked to the very far part of the bus stop.

Mark, a boy at the bus stop who also lived in my neighborhood, came up to me and screamed, "Are you okay?"

"I'm fine," I said in a hushed tone, trying not to bring attention to me from others.

"Are you sure?" he asked.

"Yes, I'm sure," I said, getting very annoyed.

"Wow, calm down; I'm just wondering because you look like ..." He paused.

"Like what?" I asked.

"Like ..." He paused again.

"Like what!" I yelled, frustrated.

"Have you been getting beaten?" he asked.

God! Is my face really that bad that people can tell? I thought to myself.

"Umm, no?" I answered.

"Oh," he said back.

"Why would you think that?" I asked nervously.

"Because my brother used to get abused by my dad, and he acted the same way as you, and those bruises can't just all happen at one time. I don't know; it just looks like it," he said shyly.

"Oh ... how old is your brother?" I asked.

"He's eighteen now; when he moved out, it was the best day of his life."

"And you didn't tell anyone?" I asked.

"No ... if we did, we would have all ended up in a foster home because our mother died three years ago."

"Oh, I'm really sorry about everything," I said, putting my head down again.

"Thanks, and I know we don't really know each other and everything, but if you ever need anyone to talk to or anything, I'm here," he added as the bus pulled up.

"Thank you ... But I'm fine ..." I hesitated to say.

Walking up the stairs, I felt as if he knew what was going on; he just didn't want to be too pushy, but my heart was scared to let him in. I had a whole bunch of what if's in my mind. So, I didn't say anything. I sat in my seat, looking out the window at the free birds flying. I wondered if that would ever be me.

As we pulled up to school and I got off the bus, I made sure to put my head down. I heard Marina screaming, "Hey," coming toward me.

"Hey," she said as she finally came close enough to see my face. I quickly put my hands over my face, praying to God she wouldn't look at my legs.

"Hi," I said back.

"What's wrong?" she asked.

"Nothing," I answered back.

I could feel her hands on mine, trying to take my hands off my face. I struggled back but failed. As she lifted my head up, the pain rushed back.

"Ouch!" I screamed; as she looked at my face, a tear ran down her face.

I was really getting tired of people crying for me. I mean, it was nice but at times very annoying.

"Oh my God! Jenny!" she screamed.

She pulled me aside to the corner and whispered, "She beat you?" All I could do was look down; I was speechless.

"Oh my God, Jenny, look at you! You look horrible," she said to me.

"Oh, thanks, that makes me feel much better," I said in a little rude tone.

"I'm sorry; it's just that you look as if someone ran over you going forty-five miles per hour," she answered.

"That's even worse, Marina!" I screamed, covering my face.

She held me in her arms, and I felt that warmth and care that I wished I had at home.

"Everything is going to be okay; I'm here for you," she whispered in my ear.

As she let go, she asked if I wanted to go to the nurse and just stay there all day. I said I did not, because if the nurse called my mom, I would have gotten double the pain I got yesterday. As the bell rang, my heart dropped. "Great," I whispered to myself. As I walked into the school, all the faces turned, looked at me, and then walked away. "At least they're not asking me what's wrong," I said happily to myself. As I walked to my first period, I kept my head down and looked up occasionally to see where I was going. When I finally got to my class, I sat down and laid my head on my desk gently. As we went over our homework, I hoped she wouldn't call on me, but I guess I didn't hope hard enough because she called on me for the very first problem.

"Jenny, can you answer number ten?" she asked. *Um, nooooo!* I thought to myself, but I ended up saying sure instead. As I did the problem, I put my head down and read, "Two *x* plus three *x* equals, um, five *x*."

"That's correct," she said to me. "But can you put your head up while you're talking? I can barely hear you."

Ughhhh! Are you freaking kidding me? I screamed in my head. As I lifted up my head, the whole class was looking at me. Their eyes got huge, as if there was something seriously wrong.

"Umm, Jenny, may I talk to you in the hall?" she asked me.

I had no choice but to stand up and follow her. As she opened the door and it closed slowly, I could hear the rumbling of the other students talking about me. A tear formed in my eyes, but I fought to keep it in and not run down my face. As Mrs. Conrad closed the door, she looked into my eyes and said to me, "Jenny, what is going on?"

"Nothing," I answered, strictly putting my head down.

"Jenny, your face is bruised up badly; how do you explain that?" she said to me, kind of yelling.

"I tripped down the stairs in my house and hit my head really hard on the banister," I lied.

"Okay? Then why are your legs all swollen, too?" she asked.

I didn't reply.

"Jenny, I'm trying to help," she said to me, lifting my head up.

"I don't need your help ... I'm fine!" I yelled, but deep down, I knew I wasn't okay at all.

I was hurting inside and out. As I opened the door to the class, they all shut up and gazed at me as I sat back down in my seat. As the bell rang, I grabbed my stuff and walked to my next class, making sure I put my head down, trying to avoid any contact from anyone that I knew would ask me what was wrong. Apparently, I wasn't paying much attention, because I bumped into about four people. I apologized with my head down and kept on my way. When I reached the gym door, that's when I put my head up, because I had Marina in that class. As I entered the gym, I made my way to the dressing room. Marina was already there opening her locker.

"Hey," she said to me in a concerned voice.

"Hi," I answered.

"How's your day so far?" she asked.

"Horrible!" I said back.

"Aw, I'm really sorry," she said, giving me a hug.

"It's okay; the day's almost over, only two more periods," I said happily.

"Do you want to sit at an empty table today so everyone won't ask you questions at lunch?" she asked.

"I don't want to take you from your friends."

"You're not!" she said.

"Okay ... If you're sure."

"I'm positive," Marina said with a chuckle.

Gym was okay, I guess. We had free gym today. Marina and I just walked around and talked. I didn't risk playing with any balls today. As gym ended quickly, we got changed, and I looked at myself in the mirror.

"Ugh, when do you think it's going to get better?" I asked.

"I don't know, maybe two to three weeks," she said. I frowned.

"But don't worry; it will be faster than you think," she added, trying to make me feel better.

As the bell rang and we walked to our next classes side by side, Marina said, "Put your head up; if it's down, people are going to want to know what's wrong with you and pay more attention to you."

What is she talking about? I asked myself, but I followed her advice anyway. I lifted my head.

"Better?" I asked with a smile.

"Yes, much!" she answered.

As we walked, I didn't get as many looks at I expected. When we got to the eighth-grade hall, I tried not to get pushed into lockers again. Marina spotted Drake and ran up to him. He hugged her around the waist, and I saw him whisper "I love you" to her. I smiled, wishing I had that, as I walked slowly, trying not to get pushed or shoved. I saw Jeremiah and quickly put my head down. As I lifted my head back up, remembering what Marina had said, I saw him coming toward me. "Great," I whispered to myself. As he came closer, I could see his eyes getting bigger and bigger with worry in them. When he finally reached me, I smiled and said hi in the most shy voice I have ever used.

He was speechless. I felt like crap; he just stood there and looked at me, saying nothing. I got too frustrated and nervous; I just walked away. He pulled me by the arm and said, "Wait."

I turned around and said, "What?" with tears in my eyes.

He pulled me over to a corner where no one was in sight. I looked at him with tears running down my face. He opened his arms and said, "I'm so sorry." I cried even harder because just being in his arms felt as though I was free of everything. I felt as if I could die today and still be satisfied.

"Shhh," he whispered into my ear. He rubbed my back up and down about seven times (not that I was counting), which made me cry even harder. When he let go, he pulled out a tissue from his back pocket. I rubbed my eyes and looked at him in amazement; good thing was he was looking at me, too.

We looked at each other for about one minute before I put my head down and asked, "How did you know?"

He wiped his eyes, and as soon as his mouth opened, "Binggg!" the bell rang.

Ughhhh, I thought in my head.

He grabbed me again and said, "We will talk later."

I nodded because I was too nervous to speak again. As he ran down the stairs, he looked up at me, and I smiled. I walked to class on cloud nine. When I turned the knob of the door, my teacher asked me, "Why are you late?"

"My locker wouldn't open," I said confidently.

"Okay, take a seat," she said to me while examining my body; for just a second, I forgot I looked horrible.

As I took my seat, I couldn't stop smiling. Marina looked at me and said, "What's the real reason you're late?"

I giggled and didn't say a word.

"You're going to tell me!" she demanded.

Again, I said nothing.

When we began to take notes, I dosed off into la la land and closed my eyes; apparently, I looked really stupid, because by the time I opened my eyes, Marina was looking at me as if I was mental. When the bell rang, Marina followed me after class, eager to know why I was late. I didn't want all my excitement and happiness to go away, even if it meant nothing to him. I told Marina I got pushed again. She asked me why I was all happy in class, and I told her a teacher saw the person that pushed me and gave him a referral. She asked why was I daydreaming, and all I could say was that he smelled really good. She looked at me, confused, and said, "Wow." Just the answer I wanted to hear. As we got to lunch, we put our bags down at an empty table way in the front where barley anyone sat. When we came back from the lunch lines, there was an extra bag.

"Whose bag is that?" I asked.

"I don't know," she answered.

That's weird, I thought to myself.

"Let's go through their stuff and try to find a name," she suggested.

"Marina, we can't just go into someone's bag and ..."

But before I could finish, she was already searching through it. She opened up a folder, and I almost crapped my pants. It said Jeremiah Daniels.

"Oh, it's just Jeremiah," Marina said and threw the backpack onto the ground. Just Jeremiah!

Oh, great, I can't eat in front of him! I can barely talk, I thought to myself, throwing my food down my throat.

"Slow down; why are you eating so fast?" Marina screamed.

"I don't know; I just feel like it." I laughed.

"Wow, you're so weird!" she said with a smile, as I swallowed and began to drink. Jeremiah and Drake walked up to the table.

Yes! Just in time, I thought to myself.

"Hey," Drake said to Marina, kissing her on the cheek as he sat down.

"Hey, Marina," he said with a smile.

Jeremiah and Drake sat in front of Marina and me. As I looked down at the table, I saw Drake looking at my forehead. I felt so uncomfortable. Jeremiah kicked him under the table, which made me laugh. When Marina left to go to the bathroom, Drake kept looking into my aching eyes. I looked at him and smiled. When lunch was over and Marina and Drake left, Jeremiah held me back and handed me a piece of paper.

I opened it ... It was his number. He looked into my eyes and said, "Whenever you need or want to talk, call me; I'll always pick up."

He rubbed my cheek where a huge bruise was and said, "I'm here for you; don't worry."

And then he smiled, as he turned around and walked away; I couldn't move. I screamed to myself and felt my heart actually smile. When I started getting the feelings back in my legs, I walked to my last period. As I walked in, I really didn't care if people looked at or talked about me. I was way too happy, but knew that as soon as the bell rang, I was on my way home, and all that happiness would soon disappear.

Chapter 5: **The Pain, Hurt, and Suffering**

On the bus ride home, I kept admiring that piece of paper that had Jeremiah's phone number on it, 259-683-1147. I treasured it, putting it deep down into my book bag in case my mom tried to go looking for something. As the bus drove from stop to stop and came closer to mine, that kid Mark came up to me and asked if I wanted to hang out today. *Yeah, right! As if my mom is really going to let me go over to your house*, I thought to myself.

"No, thank you, I'm really busy today," I answered.

"Okay, but if you change your mind, you know where I live," he said to me as we got off the bus and walked our separate ways.

"Yeah, thanks," I said with a smile, looking back.

I tried to walk as slowly as possible, so hoping I wouldn't get home, but eventually, I did. I opened the front door and closed it softly. I didn't hear anything; I was hoping no one was home … My hope was crushed when I saw everyone in my kitchen. I said hi as politely as I could. My mom glanced at me and gave me an evil eye.

"I might go outside today, if that's okay?" I asked, just wanting to get out of the house.

She turned her head quickly, as if I had asked a horrid question. I put my head down and said never mind, very frightened. I faked a smile at her as I walked up the stairs. Johnny was in my room, still in the position that I left him this morning. Johnny began to separate himself more and more from the family; he said they were all liars and mean. I walked in my room and smiled at him, saying, "Hey."

He ran into my arms, screaming, "Sissy!"

"Johnny, did you move at all from the position I put you in this morning?" I asked with a chuckle.

"Yeah, I went to the bathroom," he said with a smart tone.

"Okay, then," I said, putting my bag down.

"Why are you so happy?" he asked; there was a silent pause.

"Umm, I'm not?" I questioned.

"Oh, well, you seem like it; you're never this happy when you come home." I laughed and went downstairs.

I heard nothing but silence, so I quietly tried to go back upstairs, but as soon as I turned around and took my first step, I felt an extremely horrible pain in my back. I looked back, and it was my mother's nails clawed in my back, clenching on. Her long, sharp nails were pinned into my skin; she grabbed me from the back and dragged me to the backyard. I tried not to scream because I knew if I did, there would be an even worse punishment to go with it. As she opened the screen door, she pushed me to the ground, letting my skin go. I felt as if someone sliced my back open just a little bit with a knife. I didn't dare touch it. So, just stood there, waiting for her to bring the pain, hurt, and suffering. All I could think about was this: *Thank God she's beating me, now I can have an excuse to call Jeremiah, but would she torture me so bad that I couldn't even pick up the phone to dial his number?*

I waited and waited, my body aching from yesterday and the start of today. I waited and waited. Nothing was happening. I thought maybe this was the only thing she was going to do to me; maybe this was it. As I pulled my face up, I was very wrong. She was kneeling in front of me with the most frightening face ever. I felt as if I was in hell, and she was a demon hauting me. As I began to put my head back down, she snapped it back up.

"You of all people know that you will never be allowed out of this house! How dare you ask me such a question?"

She screamed so loud I thought my eardrums popped. I had a confused look on my face even though I knew she was talking about the whole outside thing.

"Don't look at me as though you're stupid, you dumb son of a ..." She didn't finish.

She let go of my head and looked at the door in shock. I turned my head, and Johnny was sitting down, watching, with tears running down his face. Johnny ran upstairs, and she followed, saying, "I hate you!" as she looked me straight in the eye.

I trembled as I got up slowly. I didn't know where to go. I couldn't dare go back in that house. I had to wait until Katelyn and Henry got home. I felt my back; I had two little puncture holes. I couldn't really tell if I was bleeding, but I bet I was. I stood on the porch for about forty-five minutes, praying that they would come home soon. I felt like crying, even worse dying, but I couldn't. I had to hold my head up high. It was going to be hard, but I was going to do it.

About thirty minutes later, I heard the front door open. I heard Henry laugh. My heart felt relieved; I crept slowly to the door and opened it. Each step I took hurt more and more. Katelyn came up to me and asked what was wrong. I didn't dare turn my back to her. I didn't want her to see the little red marks.

"Why are you walking like that?" she asked.

"Oh I think I cracked my back," I said, walking backward toward the stairs.

"Want me to crack it back into place for you?" asked Henry.

"No!" I shouted. "I mean, no, I don't want it to hurt even more," I quickly added.

"Okay?" he said weirdly.

As I saw Mother walking downstairs with Johnny, I quickly ran past her and up the stairs, holding in the pain. I went to the bathroom and lifted up my shirt painfully. I took a cold shower that brought so many tears to my eyes. When I got out, I stood there for a while, not wanting to move. I went to my room and put some ointment on it. I could barely bend over to my dresser to get clothes out.

Johnny opened my room door and walked in with his head down. I figured my mother had already brainwashed him.

"Hi," he said, still not looking at me.

"What's wrong, Johnny?" I asked.

"Mommy said for me not to look you in the eyes because you're evil."

Wow, my mother is so horrible; how could she tell my little brother that I was evil and that he shouldn't look at me in the eyes?

"Johnny, do you believe it?" I asked.

"No ..." he cried. I felt horrible.

My little four-year-old brother was constantly crying; he was suffering, and he'd barely even been in the real world yet. All I could do was hold out my hands and watch him run into them. I cried with him. I noticed that I cried every day, and it really pained me to see that my little brother somewhat experiences all my pain, too. As I hugged him, I wondered why my mother hated me so much. What did I ever do to deserve this? She never used to beat me until the sixth grade. I remembered the day so clearly. I came home from the first day of school telling her a guy called me pretty. She got so mad for some reason and started calling me ugly and saying that he was lying and no guy will ever think I'm pretty because I'm ugly. I ran to my room crying. I cried so hard that day because I knew from then on, nothing would ever be the same.

My mom screamed my name and demanded me to come to her room so she could clean my cut. I knew this was going to be horrible. She always tried to clean my cuts, even when they were fine. She would make it worse and then clean it. I walked over to her bed and took off my shirt. I laid on her bed and closed my eyes, getting ready for the pain. I was terrified. I stood there, waiting, until I heard her say, "Stay still; this may hurt a little," as she said all the other times.

I laid there, waiting until I felt drops of liquid hitting my back. It was burning so bad I felt as if someone was stabbing me gently. I cried so hard; the pain seemed forever. She kept pouring more and more; she didn't stop until Katelyn came into the room to my rescue and said, "Mom, isn't that enough?"

My mom looked at her, disgusted, and said, "Yeah, I suppose it is."

Then she went to the bathroom and brought back two big bandages and placed them on my back.

"There, you're all done," she said as I got up looking like a puppy that had just lot his home.

I cried deeply inside from my heart aching. I laid on my bed, stomach first, and hugged Johnny. I could tell his heart was crying, too. As he walked out of my room, I picked up the phone to call Marina; it rang about two times until I heard a hello.

"Hi," I replied.

"Jenny, what happened? I've been calling you all day!" she asked and kind of yelled.

"Oh ... You have? I'm sorry," I answered.

"Did you ..."

"Umm, yeah."

"Did it involve blood?" Marina asked.

"Umm," I replied.

"Oh my God! What did she do to you?"

I didn't feel like talking about it. So I told her that. The conversation was very short and ended very quickly. I told her I would tell her everything that happened tomorrow, but I wasn't sure I would actually have the strength to tell her.

A couple of weeks went by, and my mother hadn't beaten me; most of the time, she wasn't home to beat me. My bruises and body had healed up, but my heart would soon need to be healed.

Chapter 6: *Really!*

I woke up this morning and looked at non-hurting scars on my back. I felt the places on my skin where they used to be and had a flashback of how they got there. I looked in the mirror and smiled. My life had been getting much better. My mom was barely even home anymore, which was very good for me. Jeremiah and I had gotten very close. I left the house saying good-bye to Johnny. Scrappy had died about two weeks ago when my dad punched him in the nose, causing him to bleed to death, screaming for his life. We had a funeral for him in the park, Johnny enjoyed going on the swings. I tried not to think about it too much. It just brought tears to my eyes and more pain to my heart.

As I walked out the door, I always wondered if my day would end up being horrible. My mom had been in and out of the house lately, no one knowing where she went. She just had this devious look on her face when she came home sometimes and then just ended up leaving ten minutes later, screaming. It had been a long time since I'd gotten beaten. But I never forgot the pain of getting beaten, and I didn't think I ever would. Sometimes, I got really tired of waiting for my next beating. It had been hard to just sit around not knowing when she was coming. I was usually aware. I was so used to it that without it, I didn't really feel myself. Marina said I shouldn't worry about it, but I didn't think she understood. I mean, she had a perfect life. Well, compared to my life, it seemed perfect. I just sometimes wished I had a friend who really did understand. That brings up the subject of Mark. Mark was really a good friend. I hadn't really admitted to him about my life, but I think he knew. I felt that he really did understand because he was aware of it when his brother used to get beaten. He understood what was really going on in my heart, and sometimes, that can be a good thing and a really bad thing. He sat with me on the bus every day now and still tried to get me to hang out with him out of school, but I didn't. I don't really know why, since my mom wasn't home anymore, and I could basically do whatever I wanted. I just sometimes felt if I did ... I don't know ... I might end up ... Well, you know.

Walking to the bus stop, I thought about Johnny. He really hadn't been himself lately. He hadn't been talking, and about twice a week, he would have these horrid nightmares. He also has had a fever for about the last four days. I tried everything to help him get better, but I was not even sure if it was working. I really didn't know what was going on with him: whether he missed my mom, or whether he was just sick. I tried to ask him, but as I said, he didn't really talk anymore. I tried to get him out of my mind because every time I thought of him, I ended up crying, but I couldn't help it. My little brother was my best friend before I had any friends. I didn't know what I would do without him.

As I got to the bus stop and wiped the tears from my eyes, Mark came up to me and hugged me as he did every day. As the bus pulled up, I walked up the stairs and walked to my seat. I sat down and gazed at Mark. He looked at me and said, "What?"

I shook my head and turned to the window.

He leaned closer to me and laid his head on my shoulder.

"Man, I'm so tired," he said with a yawn.

This made me very uncomfortable for some reason. I don't know why, but the fact that he was lying on me brought butterflies to my stomach. I quickly pushed him off and said, "Well, that's too bad, isn't it," with a chuckle. He looked at me and smiled, lying the other way. The bus ride seemed longer today than any other day. When we pulled up at school, I saw not only Marina's face but Jeremiah's right next to her. I forgot about him for a second, but then seeing him made it seem as if I never did. When the bus stopped, Mark got out of the seat and let me go first. *Aw, what a gentleman*, I thought in my head. I smiled and quickly got off the bus, hugging Marina first, of course, and then walking over to Jeremiah, smiling. He pulled me over and gave me the biggest hug ever, this time about ten seconds. (Yes, I count the seconds!) When letting go, he looked at me and said, "You look very beautiful today."

I not only smiled, but I could feel my cheeks getting hotter and hotter. This obviously meant they were red as heck! I never blushed, but when it came to him, anything could happen.

"Thank you," I said with the biggest smile on my face.

Marina and Drake ran over to me and quickly began to tell me about their weekend, as they always did. It would always begin with "OMG." Then they would say, "We did the cutest thing ever this weekend."

Well, Marina would say it all, and Drake would just stand there, agreeing. I didn't really think he liked me all that much by the way he always looked at me. I mean, it wasn't really a dirty look; it was just a very strong look, and he wouldn't stop until Marina called him or something. It made me feel shy and small. When Marina was done talking, I said, "Aw, that's so cute."

But to tell you the truth, I really didn't even know what she said.

We all walked up the stairs to the hall. I really just wanted to spend my whole day with Jeremiah and not go to class. Being with him made my day so satisfied, but not being with him made it seem like an ordinary, boring day. Marina and Drake went their own separate ways; Drake looked back when walking with Marina and gave me that uncomfortable, deceiving look. I turned my head quickly to Jeremiah's locker, watching him twist the shiny green knob back and forth and back again. He looked at me and laughed.

"Are you really that interested in me opening my locker?"

"Very funny, but no, I'm just looking."

He looked at me and put a piece of my curly brown hair that was across my face behind my ear with his soft mocha hands. This gave me the biggest goose bumps ever. He continued to look at me and smiled. At this point, I really did not know what to do, so I quickly looked toward the ground. Sometimes, I got the hint that he liked me, but then at other times, I felt as if he felt we were only friends. I just wished I could read his mind. I just wanted to know what he was thinking: if he wanted us to be us, or if he wanted us to just be friends. I turned around and I began to walk getting extreamly frustrated thinking about the issue. He followed me, of course, and walked beside me. He dropped me off at class, giving another one of his hugs. I smiled and walked in. School was not really my main priority anymore. I mean, how could it be? I had to worry about my brother, my mother, and boys. Well, maybe boys shouldn't be one of them, but I couldn't help it. My grades were still the same As in every class. I had a 4.3 and began to start poetry. I loved the feeling of being able to put my feelings of things on paper. I wrote nonstop when I was bored. I bought a notebook and began my collection of poems in there.

School went by extremely fast today. It seemed as if I blinked just once and then I had already gone to all four periods and was now on my way to lunch. I walked with Marina, of course, and mostly just talked about our science test and how mad she was that she got a 78 percent and I got a 95 percent. When we got to lunch, we put our bags down and went into the lunch line.

I didn't really eat anything but Goldfish crackers and water. Jeremiah and I talked half the time at lunch. He noticed I was really tired, so he let me lie on his backpack. He rubbed my arm so softly I felt even more tired than before. I put my head up when I heard footsteps coming toward our table. I looked up, and it was Mark. He sat right next to me and smiled. Jeremiah quickly stopped rubbing my arm and stared at him.

"Hey ... umm, what's up?" I tried to ask, not in a rude way.

I really wanted to ask what he was doing here!

"I saw you and decided to come sit next to you; is that okay?"

"Yeah, that's fine."

Jeremiah stood up and moved to the other side of the table, watching him like a hawk.

"What's up, man? Last time I checked, you sit with your little geeks. So, why don't you go back over there, huh?"

"Oh my God, don't be rude; he's my friend," I said with a little attitude in my voice, kind of annoyed.

"Oh, okay, so just because he's your friend, it's okay for him to walk over here and just invite himself over, right?" At this moment, I was getting very aggravated.

"Don't be a jerk; it's a free country. If he wants to sit here, he can; Marina and Drake don't seem to mind, so why do you?"

"I'm sorry it bothered you so much; I can leave if you want," Mark said, getting up.

"Yes, please do," Jeremiah said in the rudest way ever.

"I'm really sorry, Mark," I said, so pissed off.

"It's fine; I'll just talk to you later."

When he left, I got up from the lunch table, about to walk away.

"Where are you going, Jenny?" Marina asked, not aware of what just happened because she and Drake were making out the whole time.

I walked away, and Jeremiah followed, of course.

"Don't follow me!" I screamed in his face and continued to walk out of the lunch room.

I ran up the stairs, hearing footsteps running behind me. I turned around. "What part of 'don't follow me' don't you understand?"

"Jenny, I'm sorry; I didn't ..."

I didn't dare let him finish what he was going to say.

"What the heck is your problem? What gives you the right to tell someone to leave if they come sit next to me? Not you, me! He's my friend, so why in the hell do you have a problem with it?" I yelled.

"I know; I'm sorry. I just I don't know; I didn't think when I said all those things, I just ... I don't know." He grabbed me slowly and gave me a hug, saying, "I'm so sorry; please, don't be mad at me," over and over and over. Which led me to give in.

"Apologize to him."

"What?" he asked.

"Apologize to him."

He paused and then said, "Okay."

I felt I shouldn't have given in so easily to him. I mean, he was such a jerk, but then, I also couldn't help it because I liked him so much; it was hard not to forgive him.

As I sat in my next class, I dosed off, wondering why I cared so much if Jeremiah was being a total jerk to Mark. I came to the conclusion that I was just trying to be a good friend. As soon as class ended, I walked out, and there was Jeremiah, waiting for me. He looked at me kind of shyly. I pulled him over, taking control, and gave him a hug. He asked, "So, you forgive me?"

"How couldn't I?" I asked.

We hugged again, and he walked with me to my next class.

"Hey, Jenny!" A scream came from behind me.

I turned around, and it was Mark. I smiled, looking at his bright white smile and his long, dirty blond skater boy hair and amazingly beautiful hazel eyes.

"Hey," I answered.

"I thought I might walk you to class if you want," he said with such a cute smile.

I quickly thought of Jeremiah and snapped out of it.

"Um, yeah, but Jeremiah was going to."

"It's fine; he can," Jeremiah added. I smiled. "Hey, I'm sorry about earlier today in lunch."

"It's fine. I could understand why; I shouldn't have approached your table like that," Mark said, putting his hand out.

I stood there so happy that they were getting along. Jeremiah and Mark shook hands. I had the biggest smile on my face.

I'm so happy my two guy friends are getting along, I thought, but maybe I shouldn't have thought that too quickly, because as time went by, I had Jeremiah and Mark walking me to class at the same time. Mark was on my left side, and Jeremiah was on my right. *I thought you guys were going to be friends; seem like nothing changed in about thirty minutes!* I thought to myself.

When I got to my class, I really just wanted them to both leave. I was so tired for some reason and so cranky. Jeremiah said bye to me first, hugging me and twirling me around (I think trying to show off in front of Mark); when Mark approached me, he was so gentle and sweet; he wrapped his arms around me and didn't let go. I felt so calm in his arms, and when he did let go, I wished he hadn't. He smiled and walked away. Jeremiah was standing behind a corner looking at us. I laughed to myself and walked into class.

Chapter 7: **Do I Like You?**

After the day ended, I felt so relieved. I really just felt like going home and sleeping. As I walked onto the bus, I sat in my seat (more like laid) and closed my eyes. Mark came and screamed "*Wake up!*" right next to my ear.

I jumped and slapped him right across his face. He laughed so hard he turned all red like a bright cherry. I turned back to the window, ignoring his loudness. He scooted over next to me and said, "I'm sorry; did I wake you?"

I looked into his eyes and began to laugh. The whole bus ride home, we talked. He asked if I liked Jeremiah. I told him no, and he said Jeremiah liked me. Sometimes, I really wondered how people could see these things and I couldn't. I tried convincing him that Jeremiah didn't, but he just came up with different reasons why he did.

"I mean, you're beautiful; why wouldn't he?" he said to me at one point.

I looked at him and said, "You're sweet."

"So, do you want to hang out today?" he asked, changing the subject to him.

I thought to myself, and for some strange reason, the word yes came out of my mouth. I wasn't the only one surprised, because when I said yes, he also looked shocked.

"Really?" he asked, I think wanting to make sure.

"Yes," I answered back.

We made arrangements to hang out around 6:00, since we got home around 4:30, maybe 4:45. He walked me halfway home, which I thought was really sweet, since we live on opposite sides, away from each other. He gave me a hug and told me I better not cancel on him. I smiled and turned away. I walked home joyful and excited. I really wanted to become close friends with Mark. I don't know why; I just really did, maybe because I could just really see myself talking to him about anything and *everything*, but I don't know. Maybe everything I thought we would have was just a fantasy, but I was willing to find out.

When I got home, I ran upstairs to see how Johnny was doing. He was sleeping on my bed. I walked over to him and felt his forehead; it was highly warm. I kissed him on the cheek and went to the kitchen to see if my mom was home. Thank God for me, she wasn't. I looked at the clock ... 5:00 is what it read. *One more hour*, I thought to myself, wishing the clock would run faster. I decided to get out of my clothes and find something else to wear. I ran upstairs and opened my closet. Trying to be quiet so I would not wake Johnny, I tried on about four outfits.

An orange and yellow T-shirt that read, "Ask my boyfriend," with shorts, a green flowy dress, jeans with a hot pink tank top, and a light blue V-neck with Bermuda shorts. I decided to wear the shorts with the orange and yellow shirt, just because it was about ninety degrees outside.

I looked at the clock again and it read 5:45 ... *Yes!* I thought to myself, grateful that the time had finally gone by as fast as I wanted it to go. I went to the bathroom and looked at myself in the mirror. I put my hair up in a quick bun and ran out the door. I walked down my street and turned. I saw a car speeding by me; I looked back and noticed it was my mom. She looked back at me and kept driving. I ran at this point to Mark's house, just in case she turned around.

When I got to his house, I looked at the clock above his front door that showed that it was 6:02. Perfect, I was not too early and not too late. I walked to the door and rang the bell. After about five seconds, the door opened. I saw that Mark had changed, too, because now he was wearing a blue T-shirt with white basketball shorts.

"Hey, you're late." He laughed.

I put my head down and up again, saying, "Sorry ... I didn't mean to."

He opened his door wider and asked, "So, are you going to stand out there all day or come in?"

I walked slowly into his house. It smelled of daisies and many other beautiful flowers. It was bright because the colors on the wall were so warm and peaceful. The furniture was not too fancy but homey. It looked like a real home, a quiet, peaceful environment where many people would be lucky to live. I stared around and closed my eyes, sniffing the air. When I opened them, I noticed that Mark had left. I turned my head in all directions, looking to find where he would be.

"Umm, Mark?" I said quietly, trying to preserve the quietness and peacefulness in the home.

"Come over here!" he yelled, ruining the whole experience.

I laughed in my head and walked toward his voice. I came to a white door with signs on it that read, "Keep out!" I knocked on the door and heard footsteps walk over to it. He opened it and pulled me in. I screamed and closed my eyes, falling on a rubbery, soft, water-like object. When opening them, I realized I was on his waterbed. He jumped on, causing me to jump up in the air and land back on the bed on my back. It felt kind of weird because when you laid on it, you felt as if you were sinking in the ocean (or any type of water), but you were not going into the water, just sinking.

I sat up on his bed and looked at him in amazement. He eyed me and jumped up to find the remote. He turned on his TV and handed me the remote, asking what I wanted to watch. I changed the channel to a random channel, not really caring what we watched. He looked at me, saying, "Sooooo ..."

I laid my head on his pillow, closing my eyes. He jumped on top of me, tickling me, screaming, "Oh, no, you're not going to sleep!"

I screamed with laughter.

We ended up rolling on his bed back and forth, me trying to get him off and him continuing to tickle me even when I screamed, "Okay, okay, *stop!*"

I could have sworn we were doing that for about five minutes. When he let go, I felt so sore on the sides of my stomach. I tried to get up and couldn't. So I just fell on his bed and relaxed. He laid his head on my legs and began to laugh. I smiled, having no energy in my mind to even try to laugh. We spent about an hour watching *Dora the Explorer* before he turned off the TV and said, "So ... Jeremiah?"

I tried to sit up, this time saying, "What about him?"

"Are you and him a thing now? I mean, today at lunch was really intense. It's like he doesn't want any guy talking to you or something."

My face froze, trying to decide what to say.

"Um, I don't think it's like that ... I mean, like, I really don't know ... but I'm sorry about what he said. I mean, I don't think he meant it?" I said, even confused about my words that had just come out of my mouth because I really just did not know what to say.

He looked at me and asked without looking away, "Do you like him?" I looked at him and looked down.

I was really not ready to answer that question just because of the fact of how he acted today.

"I really don't know," I answered, really hoping that that was a good response.

"Okay, I don't know how you can't know if you like someone or not," he said, kind of rudely, but I didn't take it in the rude way.

"Okay. Then tell me how I should know if I like a person or not, because basically, I do not understand, do I?" I answered, kind of snootily.

"When you look at him, does your heart drop? Do you feel safe in his arms? Can you just stare into his eyes forever and know that everything is going to be okay? Can you trust him? Do you get butterflies in your stomach when you hear his name or voice? Are you attracted to him and every part of him? Basically, do you like him?"

I looked down, feeling so weird about the conversation. The way he said all those things made me actually think that I might not like Jeremiah ... But I might like Mark. I looked at him and said, "Mark ... I don't know." And I was serious, because I really did not know anymore.

The look in my eyes was serious. I looked down again, feeling a bit uncomfortable. He turned the TV on again and turned away from me. I got up and looked at the clock. It was 8:30.

"I think I'm going to leave," I said, getting up.

He looked up at me and opened the door. I felt as if he was mad at me. It wasn't a great feeling at all, when he opened the front door. He walked out, too; he walked with me all the way home. We walked in total silence. When we got to my house, he hugged me good-bye but didn't say a single word. I walked inside, kind of sad, thinking that I had done something wrong. I thought about the things he had just said. *Do I like Jeremiah?* I asked myself over and over, trying to see if my answers to those questions were all yes, but they weren't. I didn't know if I was just making the answers no or if they really were no. As I got to my room, there was a smell that reeked of a dead person. I hesitated to go in and then remembered Johnny was in there. There was throw-up all over the floor, and even spots of blood. I threw myself to the floor and picked him up. He felt so weak and not alive. I cried to him, "Johnny, what happened? Are you okay? Johnny, talk to me!"

He opened his eyes carefully and said, "I'm sorry I threw up on your carpet." I smiled and held him close.

He coughed in my hands and threw himself back down.

"I don't feel so good, Jenny," he said, looking at me with his eyes so wide and weak.

"I know you don't. And I'm sorry; I really am."

My mom and dad hadn't been so good anymore. She would leave constantly and come back home for more of her stuff. It got to the point where most of her clothes weren't in her closet and the pictures of her in the hall were gone. My dad hadn't been home either. He would leave the house constantly for hours and not come back. Henry and Katelyn noticed, but I don't think they paid as much attention. We all barely talked. It was like my only sibling was Johnny, and now that he was sick, I felt as if I might be losing him. I really felt as though I needed to do something about this, take him to the hospital and tell somebody, anything to make sure he was going to be okay at the end of the day.

I held him close and told him everything was going to be okay and that he was going to be fine. He looked at me and had no energy to say anything back. I cried in his arms as he fell asleep in mine.

Chapter 8: **Poor Johnny**

The morning started off with me looking in the yellow pages for doctors nearby, for Johnny. We didn't have a family doctor. I don't even think I've ever been to a doctor since my birth. I found three doctors' offices, one fifteen minutes away, one twenty-five minutes away, and one thirty-eight minutes away. I wanted the best doctor for Johnny, not just the closest. I wrote down the numbers and put them in my back pocket. The bus ride to school was normal. Mark didn't sit next to me, which made me kind of upset, but I knew I would get over it. When we got to school, I walked off the bus and walked slowly over to Marina. Today was the first day I saw her without Drake at her side. Before I could even ask were he was, she told me that they got into an argument last night so they were not talking to each other. I thought that was dumb because I knew they would be all lovey dovey again by lunch, so I didn't really care that much, but I did make sure I said I was sorry and gave her a hug.

Jeremiah came up to us and smiled. I don't know why, but I really didn't even want to see his face. So when he looked at me, I looked away and told Marina I was going to the bathroom. Of course, he followed me there, and this made me even more annoyed. He called my name about three times; I kept walking. He ran up to me and asked what was wrong. I told him nothing and kept walking. When I got to the bathrooms, I turned around and said, "What, are you going to follow to into the stall, too?"

He stopped walking and just stood there.

"I'll wait then."

This made me even more annoyed. I walked into the stall, just standing there, waiting until he left. I had a feeling he was still there. I walked out and looked out the door. He was against the lockers, looking straight at the door. I rolled my eyes and walked out. He walked beside me and just kept looking at me, over and over. As I began to walk faster, he did, too.

"Did I do something wrong?" he asked, pulling me back.

I turned fiercely and said, "No, I did."

"And that would be?" he asked.

I looked into his eyes and saw love, peace, and happiness. My heart pumped because as I looked at him, I thought of Mark. I put my head down and breathed.

"Nothing, never mind."

He let go of my arm and turned the other way. I looked at him walk away from me and closed my eyes, thinking of what I did. I turned around and walked up the stairs. The bell had rang, and I quickly walked to class, hoping I wouldn't run into Jeremiah. My mind was telling me one thing, but my heart was telling me another. *You need Mark; you want Jeremiah*, and *You need Jeremiah; you want Mark*. At this point, I chose not to listen to any one of them. I didn't think it would matter anymore. Mark was already upset at me, and Jeremiah, I think, was just confused.

As I walked into my class, I took a seat. I stared at the board and yawned. I put my head on the desk and closed my eyes. The good thing about this teacher was that she didn't really care if you listened or not, and today, I really did not feel like learning, so I decided not to. When class ended, I walked out and looked both ways, making sure I didn't see anyone I didn't want to see. I just wanted the day to be over. To bad it had barely even started. When walking down the stairs, I saw Mark; he looked at me and walked the other way. I put my head down and sighed. I had a feeling I should walk after him and apologize, but then, I also thought to myself, *What do I need to apologize for?* I mean, I was being honest. If I hurt him, I was sorry, but it was not as though I did it on purpose. That's what I don't understand: every time I tell the truth, people get mad at me, but when I tell a lie, they get mad at me even more. So, I guess I shouldn't even talk anymore or even express myself. When I got into gym, Marina and Drake were at the door yelling at each other—intense yelling.

I ran up to her because she was crying. She looked at me and said, "It's fine, Jenny; don't worry about it."

I looked at Drake, and he gave me one of those weird looks I told Jeremiah about. I turned away quickly and walked into the locker rooms. I wondered why they were yelling like that. I have never seen them like that. They're always making out or holding hands. When Marina walked in, she was bawling. I walked up to her and gave her a hug. She cried on my shoulders. It felt kind of good, because it wasn't me this time crying.

"I think we're going to break up, Jenny," she said, sobbing.

I was so shocked I didn't even know what to say so I just stood there with her, holding her. I wanted to ask what was going on, but I figured if she really wanted to tell me, she would. She let go and opened her locker while wiping off her tears.

"It's whatever, I guess."

I stared at her and just stood there.

"No, it's not' you guys have been going out for, like, a year."

"A year, two months, and eight days," she corrected me.

I laughed and said, "Oh, well, I was pretty close."

She smiled and said, "Yep."

"Well, are you going to tell me why?" I asked, too impatient to wait until she told me.

"Last night, someone told me he liked one of my friends, and I don't know; I got so angry I called him and cursed him out. Then, it just elevated from there," she said, sitting down with her gym clothes in her hand. I thought to myself, *Could that friend be me? I mean, he always looks at me kind of weird, but it couldn't be*, I told myself.

"Oh, I'm really sorry. Do you know who that friend could be?" I asked.

"No ... why, do you?" she asked, getting up.

"Oh, no, I was just asking," I answered, walking over to my locker and opening it.

Gym was okay. The whole time we talked about her and Drake, though. I listened to most of the things she said and some I didn't because I was trying to figure out a problem myself. I needed to know what was going on. *Do I get butterflies when I see Jeremiah?* I thought to myself. I didn't know any of the answers, but how could I not? *Do I not know how I feel when I'm with him? How is that possible?* I asked myself over and over, trying to find an answer, but sadly, I couldn't.

After gym, Marina and I made our way to science. I walked, looking at her every second to make sure she wasn't crying. I felt really bad for her. Drake was a guy she thought she could never live without, so seeing her lose him was very sad. She walked with her head down so people wouldn't see her bloodshot eyes. I looked at her and said, "Keep your head up. If it's down, people will think something's wrong and for sure look at you; if it's up, they won't pay as much attention."

"Ha ha, I wonder where you got that from," she said, lifting her head and smiling.

We walked into class both smiling and sat down. We watched a movie today so we didn't really have anything to learn. I took out my poem book and began writing. Marina looked at me in wonder.

"It's my poem book," I said before she could ask.

"Oh," she said and laid her head on the table in misery.

The poem read:

What is like?
When you smile every minute when thinking of that person?
When you think about him all the time and don't know why?
What is like?
When you look at him and feel as if the darkest days have
been protected with light?
When you know that that person will always be there,
whether you are or not?
What is like?
Is there a like?
Does he like you?
Do you like him?
Or do you feel like the like that you thought you liked isn't
the like you wanted to like?
What is like?
Most of all ... who is the like?

When the bell rang, Marina walked out the door into the bathroom. I stood there waiting, reciting my poem over and over. I looked up and saw Jeremiah ... but was it wrong that I was kind of hoping it was Mark?

"Hey, I'm sorry about this morning. I didn't mean to walk away from you; you just really kind of made me mad because you wouldn't tell me what was wrong."

"It's fine; I don't know what was wrong with me anyway ... I guess I'm just a little confused."

He looked at me and gave me a hug. I wrapped my arms around him, asking myself these questions: *What do you feel when you're with him? How do you feel when he touches you?* Surprised, I couldn't really answer any of those questions because I don't think when he's with me. I mean, I do, but it just doesn't make sense. It's as if he puts a spell on me, and I don't know what I think.

Marina walked out of the bathroom and looked at Jeremiah and rolled her eyes.

"Did he tell you?" she asked Jeremiah.

"Yeah ... I'm really sorry."

"Why would you be? You're on his side, right?" Marina said with a snotty attitude.

"I'm not taking sides, Marina. You know you're like a sister to me; why would I do that?"

"Cut the crap. I know you better than anyone else does, and you're full of crap ... just like your best friend," she said and walked away with a tear running down her face.

Of course, I followed her because if I didn't, I would feel horrible, and who knew what she would do to herself. I ran behind her, looking back at Jeremiah, watching him walk away. He looked back at me and smiled.

Marina and I didn't eat lunch. We sat against lockers, and I let her lay her head on my shoulder and cry. I didn't really understand why she was crying so much, but I knew if I was going out with a guy for about a year and I really liked him, I would probably cry this much, too. So, I let her cry on me this time. She kept repeating to me, "Why?" And my answer was always the same: "I don't know; I'm really sorry."

Lunch went by quickly, and we got up and walked slowly to our next class. I hugged her and told her everything was going to be all right. She used to say that to me, and it always made me feel a little better. She smiled, and I watched her fade away into the crowd.

I turned around and saw Mark in the hall; he looked at me, turned around, and walked away. My smile turned into a frown really quickly. I put my head down and walked to my next class. We had a test. I sighed and got out a pencil. Lucky for me, it was language arts, so it wouldn't be that difficult. Of course, I was the first person to be done and the first person to get an A. That kind of made my day, but then, I just remembered that Mark hated me, and the pain came rushing in all over again. I wanted the day to end already so I could try to talk to Mark on the bus, maybe even to see if he would sit next to me or completely ignore me as he'd been doing.

When the day was over, I quickly got on the bus and slid all the way to the window. Mark came on the bus and looked at me, began to walk, and sat down ... but not with me, the seat in front of me. I sighed and put my head down, shedding a tear. I took out the piece of paper from my backpack, remembering about the doctors, and remembering about Johnny, which made me cry even more. The bus ride home felt very empty and quiet. I was kind of happy to go home to my baby brother, a brother that loved me and would never stop. I watched the birds fly across the window and smiled. Watching them be free and soar across the sky was so peaceful to me. They reminded me of me: always being kept in their nests, never being able to leave, until one day, their wings get strong enough that they can fly ... finally fly ... be free.

I got off the bus and didn't even think of looking at Mark. I walked home with the doctors' names in my hand, ready to call them and ask what was wrong and what I could do to help. I opened the door and ran to my room; he was still sleeping, but this time breathing hard. He woke up intensely, screamed, and began to cry. "I ... can't ... breathe," he said to me with his big eyes. I looked at my little brother in shock. I quickly ran to the kitchen and got him a cup of water. I told him to drink slowly, and try to breathe through his nose. He did what I said, and it worked a little. I laid him down and rocked him back to sleep. He looked so much better when he was sleeping than when he was awake, which was so sad. I lay with him for an hour until I knew he was asleep. When I was convinced he was, I picked up the phone and called the three doctors' offices. The first one went straight to voicemail, the second one didn't pick up, and the third one said it had not been in service for about a year. I got so frustrated I began to cry more than I've done in a long time. The worst fear that came to my mind was me not being able to help Johnny, for me not to be there one day when he really needed me, for me to lose my best friend, but I prayed, and I tried to stay faithful that he was going to be okay.

I looked down and saw the numbers Jeremiah put in my hand almost a month ago. There was some feeling in my heart to pick up the piece of paper and call him. So, I did.

I picked up the phone and dialed Jeremiah's number. He answered after the first ring.

"Hey," he said, knowing it was me.

"Hey."

"What's up? Is everything okay?" he asked, concerned.

"Yes. Everything's fine. I just ... I don't know, thought it would be nice to talk to you before I went to bed."

He didn't say anything. I cleared my throat to make sure he knew I was waiting for a response.

"Really, that's really ... sweet of you," he said, kind of shocked.

That night went well, but when I hung up the phone, I was still holding my baby brother, who looked as if he was dying slowly in my hands. I cuddled with him the whole night. I prayed and prayed, hoping that God would hear me and hopefully heal my brother. The only question was if my prayers would be answered. Or would I be left with ashes to hold at the end?

Chapter 9: **What about Jeremiah?**

This morning was nothing really special. I left a bowl of soup by Johnny's bed just in case he woke up and was a little hungry. The bus ride to school was the usual. I looked out the window and once in a while glanced at Mark to see if he was looking at me, but every time I did look, he never was. So, it got to the point where I just stopped.

When we got to school, I ran off the bus and looked for Marina, but she wasn't there. I figured her bus didn't come yet. When the bell rang, I saw Drake and Jeremiah, but no Marina. So, I went up to them and asked, "Hey, where's Marina?"

"She stayed home today," Jeremiah answered.

"Why?"

"Maybe because I was planning on breaking up with her today," Drake butted in.

"Oh," I said, shocked.

Jeremiah came over and hugged me, and I smiled when he let go. I didn't bother asking myself any of those questions because they were just making me more confused, and upset. Plus, Mark wasn't even talking to me, so I didn't really get the point of wondering if I liked him or not.

I looked up, and Drake was in front of me with his arms open. I just stared at him for a moment before I noticed he wanted a hug, too. I opened my arms and felt his hands rubbing up and down my back. This touch made me feel weird. If Marina was here, she would freak out. When he let go, I looked up, and he winked at me. I turned my head, and Jeremiah was gone. The bell rang, and Drake said, "I'll walk you to class."

I didn't want to be rude, so I didn't say anything. I tried to tell myself that he was just trying to be nice since Marina wasn't here. But I had a very strong feeling that the reason he broke up with Marina was to be with me. Well, to *try* to be with me. I walked extremely fast so the moment would end faster than it seemed he wanted it to end. When I got to my class, I said thanks very quietly and walked in, leaving him openhanded at the door. I sat in class so upset by this. I didn't want to lose Marina to gain Drake, even though I didn't want Drake. If Marina found out what I knew, if it was true, I knew I would lose her in a heartbeat. I tried not to think too much of this. If I did, problems would just arise and become worse.

After class, I walked fast to gym. Since Marina wasn't here, I didn't really do anything today but play basketball ... by myself. Every class was lonely without her, and thinking about her boyfriend having feelings for me made it even worse. I didn't eat lunch that day either; I sat in the same spot where Marina was crying on my shoulder the day before. I sat there listening to music, thinking. Jeremiah walked by and said, "I thought I'd find you here."

"How did you know?"

"I have my ways, ha ha."

He sat next to me, listening to music. I smiled the whole time he was with me. He looked me dead in the eye and told me something I think I will never forget.

"I like you, Jenny Fortella ... I like you a lot."

I looked at him and felt the passion he had for me. My heart was pumping so hard, and words weren't coming out of my mouth.

"Jenny?" he asked.

"Jeremiah," I said, putting my head down.

He got up and began to walk away. My heart stopped pumping so hard. I felt as if I was watching my dream walk away, so I got up and got the strength to say, "Jeremiah, I like you!"

He turned around ran over to me and grabbed me in his arms. I smiled, but something inside of me didn't feel complete. He leaned over and kissed me so gently and softly. His lips were moist and warm. When I felt them on mine, my heart raced so fast; it was amazing, but I still didn't feel what I thought I would. He let go and smiled. I did the same, but deep down inside, I think I was crying. I felt as though I was lying to him; more importantly, I felt as though I was lying to myself.

That day was very important. I realized that you might not always get what you want but get what you need. The day went by extremely fast, but in my mind, it felt as if every moment went by slower than ever. Jeremiah walked me to every class since the kiss. We made it clear that we were going to take things slowly, and that we didn't have a title on whatever it is that we had.

I asked myself constantly ... *Is it wrong that I'm happy with Jeremiah, but every time I'm with him, I feel unhappy, as if I need something else ... and maybe that something else is Mark?*

I tried my best to stay as far away from Drake as I could. It seemed as if every time I was with him, something unusual or uncomfortable happened, and I really didn't want to lose my best friend over something as dumb as him. How can a guy move from his girlfriend for a year to her best friend? He knew that if he did that, we wouldn't be friends anymore, and Marina was my only true friend ... so why would he do this? I thought my life was getting a little better with my mom gone and everything, but with Johnny sick, and boys, and the thought of almost losing my best friend, my days were even worse than they were when my mom was home torturing me.

After class, I walked out and saw Mark. He looked at me and walked away again, as he'd been doing. So this time, I followed him. He looked back and began to walk faster. So I did the same. I felt him getting very annoyed because he began to speed walk, and after that kind of jog; it got to the point where he was running. But I was still walking. I didn't want it to seem as if I was desperate to talk to him, but I did need and want to talk to him. So I followed, until I got to his classroom. Right when I walked past the door, he flew in. So, I turned around and walked to class; of course, I was late, though. I don't think there was a time I was not late to this class. I barely pay attention anyway, so I don't see why it matters.

When I walked in, my teacher looked at me so fiercely she began to hurt my eyes. I took my seat, but she told me to get up.

"Since you would like to be late to this class and not even pay any attention, maybe it's time you go to the office and do the same thing. I am not going to take it anymore," she said with a rude attitude.

"Fine, I'd be glad to," I said, walking out of the classroom so annoyed I really did not even care.

When I got to the office, I took a seat and did exactly what I did in that class. I stretched and laid my head on the table and thought. Thank God it was my last class. I don't know if I could handle being at school anymore. I really just needed to go home, talk to my little brother, and try to call the doctors' offices again.

When the bell rang, I felt so relieved. I got up, stretched again, rubbed my face, and walked out. I sat on the bus's black, hard, rubbery seats and laid my silky tight curls back on the seat. I looked at the people outside, walking and talking with smiles on their faces, and realized that all the kids out there were going through something in their lives. It didn't have to be big, but they were going through something, because no life is perfect. It took me a while to realize it, but I'm glad that I did.

I gazed at his tall, muscular, blond hair, and blue-eyed self when he walked on the bus. He looked at me and rolled his eyes. I looked down and smiled because even though he was mad at me, at least he took the time to look at me and do something rude. I enjoyed the beauty of the world while the bus was moving. I looked up to the sky and saw the clouds floating by, graceful and all, hoping that one day I'd be up there, too. When the bus stopped, I walked off and ran up to Mark before he could leave.

"Why ... why do you hate me? What did I do, Mark?"
He looked at me and stopped walking, turned around, and opened his mouth.
"I don't hate you; I could never hate you."
"Then why are you so mad?"
There was a pause. Nothing was said. He just looked at me right in the eyes and put his head down. I lifted up his tan smooth skin and shouted, "*Tell me!*"

He still said nothing. I let go and walked away as Jeremiah did to me today, hoping that he would see it as his dream walking away, and he did, because when I began to walk, he pulled me back and screamed in my face, "*I like you, Jenny!*"

I smiled and wrapped my arms around him so tight.

When you look at him, does your heart drop?
> Yes

Do you feel safe in his arms?
> Yes

Can you stare into his eyes forever and know that everything's going to be okay?
> Yes

Can you trust him?
> Yes

Do you get butterflies in your stomach when you hear his name or voice?
> Yes

Are you attracted to him, and every part of him?
> Yes

Basically, do you like him?
> *Yes*

And there you have it. When I was wrapped in his arms and heard those words, my mind and heart answered all those questions for me. I didn't even have to think about it, because I knew all along that Mark was my like. The only thing that crossed my mind was ... *What ... about ... Jeremiah?*

Chapter 10: **Good-bye, Mark?**

After the hug, he kissed me on the cheek (which, I feel, showed that he didn't want to take things too fast … which was good), and I walked home.

I thought about Jeremiah … *What am I going to do?* I asked myself about a million times, and still no answer. I felt like a jerk. How could I go from one guy to another? I mean, I liked Jeremiah… but I liked Mark more. I felt I had more with Mark. I could just look into his eyes and know what he was feeling. With Jeremiah, I couldn't do that. It was not that I was incapable of doing it; my heart just wouldn't let me. I walked home in confusion; my day just kept getting better and better, didn't it? First, Drake liked me (I think?); then, Jeremiah kissed me and told me he liked me; then, I got detention; and last, Mark told me he liked me … My day was great. Wasn't it?

I opened the door to my house and walked up the stairs. Johnny was still sleeping. He didn't even touch the bowl of soup I left this morning. I woke him up gently; he opened his eyes and smiled.

"Did you eat today?" I asked, concerned.

"No."

"Johnny, you need to eat!" I screamed.

"I'm not hungry," he said, about to cry, scared from my tone of voice.

I sat next to him and sang. It always seemed that made things better, and it always put a smile on his face.

"Baby boy … You need to get stronger. Baby boy … My heart is getting weaker, because you … you're not feeling well … and the sight in your eyes brings pain to my heart … So, baby boy, you need to get stronger, so I can hug you once again, with joy in your laugh and not pain."

I sang with tears in my eyes.

"Again, again!" he tried to shout.

"Okay."

So, I sang that song over and over again until he learned the lyrics and began to sing it with me. We were in my room crying, singing the song "Baby Boy," which I dedicated to him. I fed him soup later on in the night. I promised him if he ate, he would get better, so he did.

The whole night, I thought about him. I looked on diseases. com to find what was wrong with him. I found out he might have Hematemesis, which is a deadly disease that could cause death. When I read the word "death," my heart began to pump, and I began to cry. I quickly ran up to my room, grabbed the doctor's piece of paper, and called the numbers again and again. I left about four voicemails, each one crying so hard I don't think they will be able to hear me. I cried in my hands so hard I fell on the floor, cradling myself to sleep on the living room floor. I eventually woke up around midnight and went upstairs to my room.

Johnny was sleeping, holding my picture in his hand. I turned off the light and walked over to my bed, kissed his forehead, and whispered, "I love you, Johnny," in his ear. That night, I barely slept. I kept waking up to my nightmares. I rubbed my face up and down about a hundred times before I could fall back to sleep. And before I knew it, it was 7:30, which was time for me to wake up for school. I felt as if I had gotten no sleep. I woke up with bags under my eyes and wrinkles in my forehead. I tried to cover up as much as I could with cover-up, but it just didn't seem to work, and it made me look like an overdone Barbie. So I took it all off. I got dressed, went back to my room, and saw my poor little baby brother with his eyes closed, looking all peaceful and well. I dropped to my knees and began to pray, begging God not to take him away. *I cannot live on this earth without my baby brother, without seeing his face every morning, and kissing him goodnight; I just can't be here without him. So please, please, don't take him away*, I prayed over and over, crying harder than I think I did last night.

When I left for school, my face was a mess, my hair was slopped up in a bun, and my clothes ... oh, God, my clothes were a mess. It looked as if I basically got ready in the dark. But I didn't care; all I cared about in that moment was my brother, and if he didn't get better, I felt as though I would never be okay again. I walked halfway down the street, and at the end, I saw a speck: it wasn't moving; it just stood there. Not even moving a little. So I walked slower, trying to figure out was that was, but as I got closer and closer, I saw a tall blond figure and knew it was Mark. I smiled at the fact that he waited for me, but Johnny was still in my mind; that made my smile go away. I walked up to Mark, and he opened his arms and grabbed me.

"Good morning," he whispered in my ear.

"Good morning," I said back, trying to be as quiet as he was.

He let go, and I smiled.

"What's wrong?" he asked as if he could feel the pain coming from my heart.

"Nothing."

"You know you can tell me," he said, looking me in the eye.

"I know."

"Then ...?" he asked me, not sure of his words.

"There's nothing wrong ... I promise," I said, trying to act sure of myself.

He looked at me, smiled, and hugged me again.

The bus ride was okay. He laid his head on my shoulder the whole time while holding my hand. I wanted to smile but I just couldn't. Everything just kept getting worse. I was waiting for the next worst thing to happen to me.

I got to school and prayed to God Marina was there ... And she was, so my day was getting better. I didn't tell her what had been happening with Johnny, Drake, Jeremiah, or even Mark. I had not been too open lately. I felt my business was my business, and no one else needed to know.

When I saw Jeremiah, he walked up to me, and Mark grabbed me by the waist tightly ... maybe letting Jeremiah know that I was his? I quickly pushed him off and ran over to Marina. Jeremiah looked at me kind of weird, but he would get over it (I thought) ...

"Jenny! I missed you."

"I know; I missed you, too. What's been up? Why weren't you at school?" I asked, trying to find out if it was true that she didn't come because Drake was going to break up with her.

"Drake broke up with me last night over the phone ... I couldn't take watching him do it in person, so I didn't come," she said, kind of ashamed.

"Oh," I said, kind of confused why she would do that.

"I mean, I was fine with him breaking up with me ... just not in person."

But wouldn't you want a guy to break up with you in person rather than in text? I asked myself.

"Oh, I understand," I lied to her, because I did not want to seem stupid.

Both Mark and Jeremiah tried to walk me to class, hold my hand, talk to me, and even hold my books. They didn't really understand what was going on because they both showed up at the same time to basically do the same thing. One guy thought he was my guy and so did the other. I didn't want to hurt either of them, but I figured in the end, it might turn out that way.

As I was on my way out of math, Mark stood outside and waited. When I walked out, he was waiting; he looked at me, and I got the chills for a moment.

"Why is Jeremiah trying to do everything I do? Why does he keep following you around and trying to get a hold of your hand to hold it? Doesn't he know ... about you and me?"

"Yeah ... of course he does ... I'm sorry; we're just really good friends," I lied. And the reason I lied was because I didn't want to hurt Mark, even if I was hurting him more by not telling him. I guess I was willing to take that risk.

Mark held my hand during the whole day, but when I saw Jeremiah coming, I made an excuse to let go. I pretended to scratch my hand or to sneeze, but I made sure one did not see me with the other. Now, you may say I'm turning into a monster, but I was doing the best for myself, and for them.

"Need a gentleman to walk you to class?" he asked as he came up to us.

Mark quickly looked at me in anger.

"I'm sorry, but I promised him," I said with fear.

"It's fine ... as long as I get you when you get home," he said with a great big bragging grin on his face aimed at Jeremiah. As he walked away, Jeremiah talked.

"You guys hang out ... I mean, out of school?" he asked.

"Yeah ..." I said, so ashamed.

"Oh. Wow. Okay," he said, kind of disappointed that I said yeah, but what could I do?

I felt as if Jeremiah was disappointed in me, but I was already disappointed in myself, so I didn't really mind. The only thing I really cared about was myself, and my baby brother. I know that's cruel to say, but that was the truth. It was my truth.

I could tell Marina knew something was going on because after one bell, she would see me in the hall with Mark, and then after the next bell, she would see me with Jeremiah. So, she would always give me this weird look, like "What are you doing, Jenny?"

Jeremiah asked what I've been doing hanging out with Mark so much after about a couple of weeks. I told him it was nothing. But I knew it was a lie. Every night, I would go to Mark's house, go back to mine, take care of Johnny, and go to school the next day and hang out with Jeremiah. It got to the point where Jeremiah got so frustrated, he would stop making the effort to walk me to every class, instead walking me to one or two, and then let Mark take the rest of the classes. I felt bad, but not that bad. I had gotten so used to the both of them that I couldn't let any of them go. Marina and I ate lunch at a separate lunch table, and Mark ate with us, while Drake and Jeremiah sat together talking about me and Mark. I just hoped that Mark never really heard their conversations, or basically heard the truth.

After school ended, Jeremiah told me to meet him by the bottom lockers. When I got there, he looked very upset; he was mumbling something; as I walked up to him, his voice got more clear. He basically said, "I don't want you hanging out with Mark anymore."

I stood still with nothing to say. So many questions ran through my mind. If I didn't listen, would he hate me forever? If I did listen, would Mark hate me forever? And most of all, would both of these guys hate me forever when they found out how big of a liar I was?

"Jenny?" he yelled, trying to snap me out of my thoughts.

"Jeremiah, I can't ..."

"Jenny, you have to ... He has feelings for you, and I don't like that at all! Either he leaves or I do."

My insides cried out; my heart screamed no! But my mind said to agree. So that's exactly what I did.

"Okay," I said with a grin on my face and kissed him good-bye for the day.

The only problem was ... was I really going to listen to Jeremiah and stay away from Mark ... or was I going to go behind his back and possibly risk two great relationships? At this point, I was willing to do anything for the love of Jeremiah... *and* ... Mark.

Chapter 11: **She's back!**

Not being able to hang out with Mark: isn't that a little ridiculous? I thought to myself over and over, thinking about what Jeremiah had just told me.

"I don't want you hanging out with Mark."

The fact that I said yes made it even worse. I couldn't believe myself ... and I definitely couldn't believe Jeremiah. I just wondered if I was really going to go through with it and not hang out with him.

I thought about this until I walked on the bus and saw Mark in my seat, looking at me. I smiled and walked over.

"Can I sit here?" I asked, giggling.

"No, sorry, I'm waiting for someone I really like," he said sarcastically.

"Oh, really, well, then I'm sorry," I said, turning my back.

He grabbed me and pulled me into the seat. We laughed, but I quickly stopped when he said, "You are coming over tonight, right?"

"Um ..." I said, not knowing what else to say. He looked at me, and I ended up saying, "How could I say no to those pretty little eyes?"

He smiled and laid his head on my lap. I threw my head back on the seat and sighed.

What am I getting myself into? I asked over and over, but I came to the conclusion that Jeremiah wasn't going to find out if I hung out with him or not. It was not as if he lived in my neighborhood and knew exactly what I was doing all the time, so how was he going to find out? This made me feel more sure of my decision but guiltier. It seemed as if I was such a horrible person, but I was really not meaning to hurt these guys. I just really wanted both of them, and I know that sounds even worse, but I wasn't willing to lose one for the other.

When we got off the bus, Mark asked me if I wanted him to walk me home. I said no, of course, and we went our separate ways. He told me to be at his house by 7:30, and I said okay, but it seemed that every time I said okay, something terrible happened. When I got home, I ran upstairs to see how Johnny was doing. He was awake! That was my happiest moment. I ran over to him and kissed him on the cheek.

"You're up!" I said, so excited.

"Yeah ... I had to go to the bathroom," he answered with bags under his eyes.

"But you still got up; that's really good, Johnny!" I yelled again, just full of excitement.

"When am I going to go to the doctor?"

"I'm trying the best I can to find you one, Johnny, but the ones I found won't answer their phones," I said, feeling bad all over again.

"Oh ... okay," he said, getting tears in his eyes and crawling back into my bed.

I fell on the floor and said, "Johnny, I'm so sorry. I know you're hurting, and that's the worst thing that could happen; seeing you in pain brings me pain. I'm truly sorry you have to go through this." He looked at me with his big eyes and closed them, slowly and gently.

I crouched on the floor next to him with my head on the side of the bed. He began to play with my eyes, and I cried.

"Everything's going to be okay, Sissy. I promise," he said, sounding so sure.

I cried even more, not because of what he said, but because of the fact that my little brother had to go through this. He quickly fell asleep as he always did, and I got up and got ready to go to Mark's. The clock read 7:15, but my heart read, "Stay home with your little brother."

Before I left, I warmed up some food for him and put it on a stool beside my bed, hoping he would wake up and eat it. I kissed him good-bye and walked away, wishing that I stayed.

Mark and I didn't really do anything but talk, laugh, and cuddle. We hadn't really had our first kiss ... and I was glad. That was one thing that Mark didn't rush into, but Jeremiah had. Exactly when I thought things were going great with our conversations, Mark just had to mention Jeremiah. When he said his name, I got ready for the argument we would soon have and stood up.

"Why is he always around?" was one of his questions, and I directly answered it like this: "Because he's my friend; you don't see me telling you who to hang out with and who not to, or ask you why you're hanging out with girls all the time."

"But that's the difference. I don't hang out with girls all the time ... because the only girl I want is you," he said, kind of frustrated at this point. I knew that that was true, so I didn't say anything back.

"Jenny," he said, grabbing my hands and holding on to them so gently and softly. "I like you ... a lot. I don't want anyone getting in between that. It took you forever to accept me into your life, but it could take seconds for me to be out of yours," he said, trying to be sincere but honest. I really didn't know what to say to that, because at that point, I really just wanted to tell him what had been going on. But then again, I just really couldn't, and I needed him to accept that, and if he didn't, then I knew I was going to loose him. The only thing I could say was okay.

When he walked me home that night, holding my hand, I wondered if it was too late to tell him about Jeremiah. I just wanted to be honest with him and let him know that I didn't want anything to happen to our relationship. But I figured if I ever told him our relationship would be over. So I didn't really have anything to say.

When I opened the front door, he blew me a kiss, and I smiled. I watched him walk away through my window upstairs. At that point, I really didn't know if I wanted to even like Mark or Jeremiah, because liking both was killing me, and only liking one would be even worse. So, I decided to make up my mind tomorrow at school and tell them both at the same time what I'd been doing and how sorry I was, and I was planning to just suck it up if they told me they hated me, or they never wanted to see me again. Anything that it was going to be, I was ready. I had to be ready. I got myself into this, so it was time I got myself out.

I slept next to Johnny, hearing him weep. I wondered why something like this happened to him ... It should have happened to me. He didn't deserve that. If anyone did, it would be me at that point or my mom. Anyone but Johnny: he was the kindest boy you could ever meet, with his outgoing personality and his amazing big brown eyes that sparkled when he was happy. He made every day of his life special;

whether he was stuck in the house all day or just hanging out with me, he always tried to have a great time. I fell asleep wondering if Johnny was happier when he was sleeping than when he was awake at that point, which was sad because a little boy should love to be awake, but he seemed so much happier when he was sleeping. I just wished I could switch bodies with him for a day and feel what he was feeling.

That morning, I got up and tried to get the energy to go to school. Mark didn't wait for me today. He wasn't even at the bus stop, or at school. I wondered what happened; if he wasn't going to be at school today, I thought he would tell me ... I guess not. Marina walked up to me all excited this morning, as if she just had a bag of candy.

"Hey?" I asked, kind of concerned.

"Hey!" she screamed.

"Okay? What's wrong with you?" I asked, not really in a good mood.

"Drake and I talked last night ..." she said, all bubbly.

In my mind, I quickly changed from bummed to happy, because I thought they got back together, which meant I didn't have to worry about him liking me or anything. So I got extremely happy.

"And ...?" I asked, excited.

"He told me he's going to tell me who he dumped me for ... or who he likes!" she said, screaming, jumping up and down. My heart dropped, and my bad mood came back in an instant.

"What! Why!" I screamed.

"I don't know ... maybe because I begged him," she said, so proud of herself.

"Why would you do that ...? Then you're just making yourself seem desperate," I said, not thinking before I opened my mouth.

"Oh … well, thanks?" she asked more than said, and at that point, I didn't even care.

Jeremiah and Drake came up to us and smiled. Drake and Marina hugged, and I watched, so disgusted. Jeremiah looked at me and asked what was wrong. I told him nothing, of course, and hoped he would leave it at that. The day went by extremely slowly, and I got more depressed after every class. Mark was still not at school, and that made me more upset. *The day I decide to be honest and truthful, he isn't here*, I thought after everyclass. Jeremiah was happy about the idea of Mark not being there, and I figured he would be, but I didn't really even talk to him either. I completely ignored him after every class, and when he gave me a hug, I only wrapped one arm around him.

At that moment, you could tell I didn't even want to live. I loved the fact that I was watching my life pass by because I felt as though in a couple of days, I would have no life.

I saw Marina and Drake in the halls a couple of times, but I never really saw them talking about whom he liked but about stupid things, like "Where'd you get that shirt? It's so rad." *Who even used the word "rad"?* I thought disturbed.

During lunch, I ate by myself in a little ally behind small little lockers that Jeremiah showed me. I just really felt like being alone. Marina called my name a couple of times, but I never answered. I didn't want to see her, hear her, or even talk to her. It was just not my day. Everything was going badly. I didn't get the chance to tell Jeremiah and Mark that I'd been using both of them just because I didn't want to let either of them go.

The only thing that was on my mind that really kept me moving during the day was my little brother.

I felt that if he wasn't in the world, I would have lost myself. I remember when he was born, and I looked into his eyes. I knew he was going to grow up to become my best friend. He was always there when no one was, he knew how to make me laugh and for sure knew how to make me cry, but I always loved him. He was my rock.

After lunch ended, I walked to class with my head up high but my heart down low. My day was long but still not over. Marina asked me if I had any idea who Drake might like. I lied and told her no, because I really did not know if it was me or not. After school, while walking to the buses, Marina and I heard, "Fight!"

"Come on; let's go see who's fighting!" she screamed excitedly.

"Ugh, okay," I said, not in the mood, but I just went because she wanted to.

When we were getting closer, we heard more and more of the same things: "Fight, fight, get him!" So I figured two guys were fighting, but who?

When Marina got all the way in the front, I heard her scream, "*Oh my God!*" I quickly ran to see who it was, and when I did get there, I was so surprised, because the two guys fighting were Jeremiah and Mark. I screamed *stop* over and over with tears running down my face, but none of them would listen. I turned around and saw the principal behind me, trying to get through.

He brutally ripped them apart and said, "*In my office, now!*"

They stopped and got up. Jeremiah's eyebrow was busted open with blood rolling down his face. Mark's nose was bleeding, and his lip was cut open. They looked around and quickly got to me. Tears were rolling down my face, and I said so quietly, "Jeremiah, Mark, I'm so sorry. I was going to tell you ..."

Before I could finish, Jeremiah walked away, saying, "I don't have time for this," bumping into me on purpose. Mark just looked at me and was shaking his head.

"And to think I fell for you?" He wiped the blood off his face, walked away, and rubbed it on the back of my shirt. I fell on the floor crying. Marina was still in shock after what had happened, and I didn't think she really noticed me on the floor bawling. I got up when I heard the gossip about to begin.

"I think they were fighting because of her," one kid said.

"Wow, she's a freaking' jerk," said another.

By the time I got on the bus, everyone knew the whole story and just sat there, looking at me as if I murdered someone, when all I did was lie. But I guess the saying was true: when you lie, you steal; and when you steal, you kill; and when you kill, you end up in jail. All that seemed true because my heart felt as if it was in jail and would be there for an extremely long time.

The bus ride home was terrible: people coming up to me, asking me questions about the fight, how I felt about it, why it happened. All I could say was "I don't know." When I got off and looked back up at the bus, all eyes were still on me.

I walked home so happy I was out of that misery but still upset that everything that happened was my fault. I wondered how Mark had gotten to school, why he wasn't there for half of the day, what started the fight, who started the fight, whether they knew everything, and most importantly, whether they would ever forgive me.

As I walked down the street, I noticed a car in my driveway. My heart paused and then began to rise. As I walked closer and closer, I noticed it wasn't just any type of car, but that it was my mom's car. I walked slowly and hesitated to go in, but realizing that Johnny was inside, I ran in and looked around. She was in the living room, throwing pictures across the hall and cursing. I tried to quietly walk upstairs, but she somehow noticed me.

She quickly turned her head, and I began to sprint upstairs, dropping everything and just focusing on running. She sprinted behind me like a cheetah and caught up. Before I even reached the bathroom, she grabbed my shirt and pulled me down the stairs.

In a long time, I forgot the feeling of being so scared you wished you were dead, but now that she was back, that feeling rushed back in as if it never even left.

Chapter 12: **Not Even Friends?**

As she pulled me downstairs, I looked up at her face and saw scars, deep bloody scars that couldn't have been done by herself. She dragged me by my shirt, and then my hair, and even my legs.

I always wondered where she got all the anger that she did have, and why she always took it out on me.

"How have you been, Jenny? Did you miss me?" she asked in a devious voice.
I said nothing.
"I bet you missed my touch, didn't you!" she screamed, grabbing my hair. All I could do was do what I was known for ... cry. She slapped me across the face and threw me on the couch. I looked up at her, and she smiled, with tobacco overgrown in her teeth. I smiled back, but that just led to worse things. She grabbed my arm and twisted it so hard and fast. I blinked at her, opened my eyes, and saw the bone sticking out. I screamed out, and the grin on her face turned into a frown; she pulled me up and hugged me. I haven't felt a decent touch from her in a long time.

"I'm so sorry," she said with a tear running down her face. But the pain in my arm was so intense I didn't really pay attention to anything she said. I felt as if someone took my elbow and slammed it on a cement road. The tears were coming down my face so hard I didn't know how to make them stop.

"*Ouch!*" I screamed over and over so she got the point that my arm hurt that badly. She quickly ran over to her medicine closet and wrapped a cast around it so tightly it hurt even worse. I screamed, and for once, the look in her eyes was sorrow. She kept repeating that she was sorry, but every time she said it, it made things worse.

When she was done, she wiped my tears and sat me down, propping my arm up with a pillow. The pain rushed down, and the tears began to stop, but the thought of Jeremiah and Mark brought the pain back. The tears came rolling down again, and my heart started to break.

"I'm sorry; I didn't mean ..." she said with tears in her eyes, and then she stopped. She ran into her room and slammed the door. I could even hear the little switch in the door lock ... meaning she locked the door, too. I looked at my arm and saw it beginning to swell; the misery in my eyes was so cold and harsh. My mind ached from all the thinking about friends, boys, and most of all family. I tried to focus just this once on myself, but I couldn't; I walked upstairs carefully with my arm up, trying not to feel the pain. I thought if I told myself it didn't hurt, maybe it wouldn't, but of course, that didn't work for me either.

When I opened my room door, Johnny was sitting up. We didn't have to talk because he knew what had happened. He struggled to stand up; falling on the floor, he crawled over to me and hugged my legs. I tried my best not to cry, but knowing myself, that could never happen. I felt as if my life got worse every day. I didn't even know if I had the strength to move, eat, or even close my eyes to go to sleep, because it seemed that every day of my life when I woke up, something worse happened to me, something that would change my life forever. I never had a day that I didn't have to worry. Every night before I went to sleep, I always thought of what I had to worry about, what was going to happen the next day, would I still be alive, or would I not even have the strength to be alive anymore.

I leaned over and tried as hard as I could to pick Johnny up with one hand, but I couldn't succeed. I fell on the floor about three times and still no accomplishment. I sat next to him and laid my head on his shoulder. He played with my hair, with his tiny swollen fingers. I looked into his eyes and felt warmth, courage, strength, and love. I wondered what he saw when he looked into mine. All I knew was when I looked in the mirror, I saw fear, I saw hatred, I saw coldness, and I saw a tiny pinch of love for my brother. *That was the most terrible thing you could see in someone's eyes ...* I thought, but I always thought it was okay, that it was normal.

But after today, I knew that it was not normal; after that day, I knew that something had to change. The only question was how it would change, when I just lost Jeremiah and Mark ... and soon Marina. I didn't know how I could change my life from being despised with hate to full of love, when all the people I loved would soon not feel the same way.

That night, I don't think I really slept. I laid there with my eyes wide and my heart shattering into little pieces. I laid there with an open mind on all my situations; I wished I could solve it ... but I couldn't. I wished I never started it ... but I couldn't go back in time and change it. I prayed that God would forgive me because I knew that no one else would. I prayed that he would guide me into a great direction and wouldn't let me down. I laid there and hoped that everything would be okay, that I would survive the next day, that I would make my life fulfilled with joy. Everything I was saying was coming out of my mouth so easily, but I knew that when it came to the fact of me doing these things, it wouldn't be quite that easy.

So, I laid there. Hoping, praying, and wishing. I even repeated these things over and over and over in my head; I just wanted them to come true. I wanted to be a changed person, and not to feel as I did when my mother was around, and not to hurt anymore ... physically and mentally. I wanted to be strong, and I really did want people to see warmth, courage, strength, and love in my eyes.

And I feel asleep repeating these thing and hoping they would come true, and I woke up the next morning feeling that it had; I just wondered if it would last.

I woke up not noticing that I could only really use one hand properly. So when I went to reach for the door with the other hand, I had an excruciating pain come over me. I had to do everything with the opposite hand, and that was really new for me. I never really brushed my teeth with my left hand, and doing my hair with one hand made it even worse. It really stunk that I didn't have anyone to help me, but I was used to it, so I didn't mind that much.

Walking to the bus stop, I made sure I held my head up high, and I knew that I wasn't going to let any guy get in my way to fly. I walked with courage, but when I got to the bus stop and saw Mark, my courage slowed down a little and my heart sped up. He didn't even notice me. He did not look at me, glance at me, nothing. He just stood there with his head down low, and when he heard the bus coming, he began to walk. I expected something bad, but I never thought he wouldn't notice me, even just a little. It was as if I didn't even exist anymore.

Walking on the bus, I looked at him about four times but still … nothing. No look, no glance … nothing. I sat down and tried to accept that everything was done, our relationship, and sadly, our friendship. I just wondered how it would be with Jeremiah.

When our bus got to school, I saw Marina. No Jeremiah and no Drake. So, I was kind of happy I didn't have to approach them. I walked up to her and she nodded.

"What's wrong?" I asked her, because she seemed upset.

"Nothing … Just that Jeremiah won't talk to me because you broke his little heart. And now Drake won't either," she said with an attitude.

"Ugh. Okay, I'm sorry, I just …" I started to say before she interrupted me.

"How could you do that to him …? He is so nice, and you decide to play him?"

I didn't understand why she was so mad. It's not as though I did it to her, and if she was me, she would have probably done the same thing.

"You don't know the whole story."

"Well, I have time. Maybe you should tell me."

I felt as if she was interrogating me, when it was surely none of her business. So I didn't say anything, and I walked.

"Wow, really?" she yelled.

I turned my head and nodded.

The whole day was mostly like that. Marina and I barely spoke, and I didn't really see Jeremiah around. The first three periods sucked because all Marina was doing was making me feel even worse about myself, and the fact that I didn't get the chance to talk to Jeremiah about it made it even worse.

Everyone was looking at me as if I was such a bad person when I walked through the halls. And when I sat down in class, even the teachers nagged me. One even said, "So, I heard you're the person who likes starting problems between guys, huh?" All I could do was look at her and smirk.

I loved that the whole day, no one even noticed my arm, or the pain that I had dealing with people pushing me and hitting my arm on the walls on purpose. I just wished I could shout out, "*I'm sorry!*" But I knew if I did that, it would probably not even help. It was going to take years for people to get over this. I just wanted people to understand, but I doubted they would because not even Marina understood, and she was my supposedly best friend. The day went by fast, but lunch was the worst. I went to sit next to Marina, and I saw Jeremiah. I put my stuff down, and she moved it and said, "Sorry, but maybe you should sit somewhere else." I looked at her and then at Jeremiah. A tear streamed down my face, and I ran out quickly enough, because if I was in there another two minutes, there would have been a tear bath in the middle of the cafeteria floor.

I walked up the steps and heard a scream behind me. I turned around, and Jeremiah was outside of the cafeteria running toward the stairs. When he got to me, he wiped my tears and said, "I know it's going to be hard for you, Jenny. I just can't do this anymore; I can't trust you, and I'm even surprised that I'm looking at you right now. I never really liked a person as much as I liked you, but the fact that you hurt me the way you did makes it even worse."

I put my head down and watched each drip of tear drop on the floor. I lifted my head up and tried to stay calm.

"Jeremiah, I'm truly sorry; I didn't mean to hurt either one of you ..."

"But you did ... I don't understand why you did. If you liked both of us, you could have said something, instead of making me look like a complete idiot."

"I know ... I'm so sorry. I really am," I said, sobbing.

"And I forgive you ... I just ... I'm sorry, but I just can't be anything to you anymore," he said with tears in his eyes. I watched his eyes, carefully, watching each tear stream down his face.

"Not even my friend?" I asked, hoping he would say what I wanted to hear, but he didn't.

"No ... I'm sorry," he said and opened his arms. I was guessing this was a good-bye hug, but I really wished it wasn't.

And I really wished everything hadn't happened like this. I wrapped my arms around him (well, one arm) and just cried. He rubbed my back and let go quickly. I wiped the tears off my face and looked into his precious eyes. I saw pain, hurt, betrayal, and hatred. He stood there and looked at me until one more tear ran down my cheek; he turned around and walked away.

At this point, I really did want to run behind him and get on my knees, begging him not to leave. But I knew it would just make things worse, that I would look like a complete idiot, and he would never forgive me. I just really didn't understand how you could be there for someone for so long and tell her that you'll always be there, and that you'll never give up on her, and then you just leave. You go and leave her standing watching you, knowing that she cares about you so much, and that she never wanted to lose you, but she did.

How could you just extract her out of your life forever during her worst time in her life? How could he just leave when I really did need him the most? Just how? I had so many questions I wanted to ask him, but I knew I would never have the chance to do so.

So, I stood and watched one of the most amazing guys walk away from my life, forever. I just wondered what was going to happen with Mark. I predicted that I would be crying twice as hard later today. I just hoped he wouldn't yell at me too much, because Mark was very different from Jeremiah ... very different. When the bell rang, I quickly ran to class, trying not to be late and trying so hard not to see Mark. Marina walked in and asked me a whole bunch of questions, of course, about Jeremiah and what he said, how he said it, did I cry, did he cry, and a whole bunch of other nonsense. I didn't tell her exactly what happened, but I told her some, because if I didn't, I wouldn't hear the last of it.

"So, have you talked to Mark?" she asked, completely out of nowhere. I had a puzzled look on my face because we never talked about Mark, but I answered anyway.
"Umm, no ... why?"
"Oh, just wondering."
I looked at her, confused and annoyed.

After class, Marina and Drake met behind the stairs. I didn't know what they were talking about, but all I knew was that when she came up, she was crying. I looked at her, and she shook her head.

I got very nervous and sweaty all of a sudden.

"Thanks for stealing my boyfriend!" she screamed across the hall, and all I could do was have a grin on my face as symbol of nervousness. My heart dropped, and I felt as if my soul had just died.

Too bad it wasn't over.

Chapter 13: **Love, Mom**

"Marina!" I yelled, running behind her, trying to figure out what to say.

"What!" she yelled, turning around.

"I'm sorry; I didn't want you to get hurt."

"So, you knew ...?"

"I thought he did, but I wasn't sure."

"But you had a clue that it was you; you lied to me," she said.

"I know, and I'm sorry; I really I am," I said, trying my best to make things better.

"Jenny, of all people, I never thought it would be you, and I never thought you would be the one to lie to me."

I put my head down and looked up again; trying so hard for her not to say the words "I can't trust you."

My heart cried when I heard those words again. Do you know what it's like to have two people you truly care about and love tell you that they cannot trust you anymore?

I was waiting for her to say the worst of it all; I didn't have to wait that long for her to say what I expected ... but did not want.

"What's a friendship without trust?" she asked.

I looked at her and shrugged my shoulders.

"It is nothing, Jenny ..."

I looked at her and sighed.

"I'm sorry, but I can't be someone's friend who lied and whom I can't trust." She turned around and walked away, leaving me behind, not knowing what to say or do next.

"Oh ... I would feel sorry for your hand, if you hadn't stolen my boyfriend," she said, turning around and frowning.

At least someone finally noticed my hand, I thought to myself, but I didn't want it to be noticed in that way. After every class, I thought about what I had done, how many people I had hurt, and what I could do to fix it. I wanted to write Marina an apology letter; I didn't think it would make a difference, but I did anyway. I knew from the bottom of my heart I wasn't going to get Jeremiah back, but I had a slight hope that it might be different with Marina.

We'd been through so much I couldn't let it go. I couldn't let her go. She was my best friend—most of all, a sister I wished I had.

So, during my next class, I wrote. It began like this:

Marina,

I am very sorry for everything I've done. I know I hurt you, but you have to understand that I didn't mean to. I had a feeling that Drake liked me, but I wasn't sure; that's why I didn't tell you. I didn't want to hurt you ... But I guess it's too late for that. I know you said you can't trust me anymore, but I will do anything to gain your trust back. I don't want my best friend to be mad at me. We have been through so much; I don't understand how you can give it all up. You are like a sister to me. I am truly sorry. Please give me another chance.

Sincerely, Jenny

Now, I felt so great about that letter, but I would soon learn that maybe it wasn't the best choice to do for her to forgive me. After class, I ran out the door and looked both ways, seeing if Marina would pass by. She didn't, so I walked out the doors to the lockers to see if she was there. She wasn't, so I went into the bathrooms to see if she was there, and she wasn't. I was beginning to get very frustrated because everywhere I looked, there was no Marina in sight.

As I was beginning to give up, I saw her getting a drink from the water fountain. I ran up to her and handed her the note. She read it right in front of me with different expressions on her face. Her eyebrows would make these weird, awkward movements, but when she was done, she looked at me, smiled, and looked as if she really liked it.

Too bad she didn't. She smiled and ripped it up into little shreds right in front of my face. I looked at her and picked up the pieces from the ground. She walked around me and stepped on my fingers.

"Oops." I looked at her walk away with a disgusted look on my face. I never thought a person who seemed so nice and friendly could be so evil and rude. I never thought Marina would be as mean as she was right now. As she walked away, I thought of all the things I had told her, and how fake she really was. I wondered if she would tell someone about my family. Thoughts ran through my mind that made me more frightened than the fact of losing two great people.

Mark walked by when I was picking up the scraps of paper of the floor. I looked up, and he was standing there. I smiled, hoping he didn't hate me, too.

"Hi," I said, so shyly.
"Can you move …? I'm trying to get a drink of water."
"Oh … sorry," I said, getting up from the floor and walking away. My eyes were all out of tears, so I didn't have the strength to cry, but God knows I wanted to.

The feeling I felt inside was lost. I didn't know how to explain it, but I knew it was there. I felt my heart beating, but it was as if it wasn't even alive anymore. I hoped for forgiveness, but I was never given it. I knew that if it was them in that situation, they would want forgiveness, too. My world felt so empty knowing I didn't have anybody. I felt so lost in the world. I kept telling myself that everything was going to be okay. That I was a strong person and could deal with this, but I knew deep down inside I couldn't.

I went through so much in my life that when it started to become better, I took it for granted. I felt as if God was punishing me. I had no one. I was a nobody. Nobody cared; no one really wanted to care.

I sat in class looking at the board. I thought about everything I had, and everything I did have. It seemed that all the things I had in the past were more than all the things I had that moment. I just waited, a little bit longer, until my world was gone. I saw no reason to live, but most of all, no reason to want to live.

So, I just sat there … waiting. Hoping that God would take me already. Hoping that he would see how miserable I was and take me, but it never happened. My dream of life never came true.

After class ended, I walked into the hall fast so no one else would see my misery. My day went by quickly, but everything that happened ran through my head slowly. The bus ride home was nothing but sorrow. I looked at Mark the whole time, wishing he looked back … he never did.

Getting off the bus, I realized that I had lost everything … The only thing that was left was Johnny, but how long would he be left for? As Mark walked past me aggressively and fast, I ran up to him and pleaded.

"Please don't hate me."
He looked at me and frowned.
"Jenny, I don't hate you."
I smiled.
"I just don't like you, so leave me alone," he said, walking away.
"Mark!"
He turned around, annoyed.
"You're all I have left … please, don't leave."
He turned back around and walked away.

I sat down on the cement road and watched him walk away into the distance. Knowing I couldn't do anything about it killed me, but I guess I had to just let it go, let everyone go that was in my life and wasn't anymore. My life changed more and more every second that I breathed. I wished so hard that it didn't, but it did.

Right now, I didn't think I could do anything about it. And I didn't think I had anything to live for anymore, but as I stood up, I reminded myself that I had one person left, so I walked home trying to put a smile on my face, but after a while, it would just turn into a frown when I thought about everything that had happened.

When I got home, I opened the door and heard nothing but silence. I walked around and noticed no one was home.

"Hello!" I yelled, seeing if I would get a response … I didn't. I put my stuff down and walked upstairs, remembering that this was where my mom began to hurt me more than ever yesterday. When I got to the bathroom, I walked in, remembering that this was where I looked at myself that one afternoon when my mother had punched me in the face. I remembered counting to seven.

I touched the mirror gently, remembering the first time I called myself beautiful. A tear fell down my face, and I walked out, closing the door, remembering the memories.

As I walked up to my room door, I saw a folded piece of paper taped to my door that read, "Mom." I opened it and began to read.

Jenny,

I have always loved you so much. You are one of the best kids a mother could ask for.
I am so sorry for everything that I have put you through; I know you have a lot of pain in your heart from me.
I never meant to intentionally hurt you.

To tell you the truth, I never thought that I would ever treat you the way that I have.
You see, your father abuses me, but from afar.
So, you guys never really saw the marks on my body because I always tried not to show my pain.
I guess I took my pain out on you.
I don't know why it had to be you ... but it was.
But I'm gone now; your brother and sister have come with me.
Your dad has you and Johnny now.
I'm sorry I left you, but I knew you would be in better hands with your dad.
Don't ever forget that I love you very dearly.
Take care of your baby brother.
I hope that one day; he can have the strength that I see in you.
I love you, Jenny Fortella, so much.
Love, Mom

I read that with tears streaming down my face. I stuttered while reading the parts about why she abused me so much. In my mind, I kept telling myself that she loved me, but if she really did love me, why did she leave? I did love my mom; reading that letter made me love her even more. I didn't know what to say or even think of the fact that my dad had me and Johnny. I had so many questions to ask.

Why are you leaving?
Why did you take Katelyn and Henry but not Johnny?
Where has Dad been?
Where are you going?
Will I ever see you again?

I got up and ran into Katelyn's room and saw nothing there but her bed. I ran past the bathroom, all the way down the hall into Henry's room, and saw the same ... nothing.

I walked slowly into my room and saw Johnny. He was as still as a rock. I walked up to him and kissed his forehead, and he felt as cold as ice.

"Johnny?" I said, softly but worried.

There was no answer.

"Johnny!" I screamed.

Still no answer.

"Johnny, oh my God, Johnny!" I screamed with tears running down my face.

No answer.

I began to shake him. He did nothing.

I laid him down and even began to pinch him.

Still ... nothing.

I began to scream over and over.

"Help!" I cried. "*Help!*" And I cried some more. I reached for the phone to dial 911, but before I could call it rang.

"Hello!" I screamed.

"Hello, this is Amy from general hospital. You called last week?"

My heart dropped, and I hung up the phone.

"Johnny, please," I yelled in his ear, hoping he was just in a long dream.

He did nothing. His eyes were shut tight, his face was pale and looked as if it was turning blue, and he felt so miserably cold.

I cried and screamed at the same time, holding my little brother in my hands, rocking him back and forth, and back and forth. I began to sing, but it seemed as if it never worked. I cried until he was soaked with my tears. They dripped onto his face and faded off after a couple of seconds. All I could think at that moment was *Why?* I didn't know what to say but "Please, come back." And I knew that wasn't going to happen, so I didn't know what else to say. I whispered, "I love you," over and over and over into his ears, still rocking him back and forth, and back and forth.

Now everything was gone: my brother, Jeremiah, Marina, and Mark. I put my brother back onto the bed and walked down to the kitchen, grabbing the bottle of Vicodin, which was said to be a pain reliever. I walked over a little more to the knife drawer and grabbed the sharpest one I could find.

I must have taken about fifteen pills that day, and my brain felt as if it was going to explode. I walked up to my room (more like limped) and opened the door.

I stood there, trying to not fall back; with my hand already broken, I didn't want to break anything else; the only thing I wanted to break … to be over, was my life. At that moment, I was going to do anything to make it happen.

I had the knife, I had a body full of pills, and I was ready to die. I figured there was nothing to live for anyway, so why not end my journey here? I raised the knife up into the air and sternly shoved it through me. My head tilted back and my body shook. I felt a sharp pain thrusting in my body. I was just so high on pills that I didn't know where, but I could feel it, and I could see blood gushing through as I collapsed onto the hard tile floor and heard the locks of the front door begin to open. My heart felt as if it was slowing down to a complete stop, and I listened carefully to the locks twist open … one, by one, by one.